FOOTPRINTS
in TIME

FOOTPRINTS
IN TIME

Petru Popescu

LAURA GERINGER BOOKS
An Imprint of HarperCollins*Publishers*

Library of Congress Cataloging-in-Publication Data
Popescu, Petru, date
   Footprints in time / by Petru Popescu. — 1st ed.
      p.   cm.
   Summary: While Jack is visiting his father, a research scientist in Tanzania,
their plane goes down over the savanna, killing everyone but Jack, who meets
a mysterious creature who helps him survive. 3856 3713   10/08
   ISBN 978-0-06-088399-7 (trade bdg.) — ISBN 978-0-06-088400-0 (lib. bdg.)
   [1. Survival—Fiction. 2. Prehistoric peoples—Fiction. 3. Tanzania—Fiction.
4. Science fiction.] I. Title.
PZ7.P7942Fo 2008   2007024599
[Fic]—dc22   CIP
                                                                       AC

Typography by Carla Weise
1 2 3 4 5 6 7 8 9 10
❖
First Edition

*To my twin brother, Pavel, who died
at age thirteen in Communist Romania.
We went lion hunting once.*

PART 1

RUAHA PARK,
WESTERN TANZANIA

CHAPTER ONE

Jack Conran lay in bed, concentrating on falling asleep, but just when he had almost drifted off, he bolted up. Predators were hunting right outside the research center's dorm.

The thirteen-year-old boy listened, his heart pounding when a herd of buffaloes bellowed as they were ambushed. Their attackers snarled and roared. Then lions landed their prey: one buffalo, its voice very loud and frightened. The snarls and roars seemed to gang up on the bellowing, as if the sounds themselves were predator and prey.

The scientists' dorm was an old structure, with cots lined up against a windowed wall. The cots had mosquito nets, which seemed like an exaggerated precaution, since the windows were wired. In the bed next to Jack's, his father opened his eyes.

"Hey," Alan Conran whispered.

The bellowing outside turned into a death moan as the lions' thrashing grew even louder. Jack looked around. He could see the other beds, occupied by his father's colleagues, who were sleeping soundly.

"You'll learn to sleep through it," Dad reassured him.

"Sounds like it's happening right outside," Jack muttered. He didn't want to appear frightened.

"It's miles away," Dad whispered. "There's a night wind that blows over from an enormous crater in the savanna—the Witch's Pot. Amazing how it carries sound. Don't worry—the lions don't hunt so close to the center. They're not stupid. Go back to sleep."

"Could those be lions that you already tagged?" Jack asked.

"No, the tagging area is much closer to the Pot's

4

rim. The lions there are isolated—they've never even seen a hunter, or worse, tourists filming them from planes. Now lie down and close your eyes, okay?"

"Yeah," Jack muttered.

Jack watched Dad settle back into his bed, his face illuminated by moonlight shining through a window screen. Three years earlier, Jack's mom and dad had divorced. Now Jack lived with his mom in California while his dad, a professor and scientist who specialized in human evolution, spent most of his time doing research in Africa.

The wind was gusting, and Jack could still hear fierce snarls in the distance.

"What's happening now?" Jack asked.

"The lionesses are fighting to see who gets the best of the kill," Dad said. "Young lionesses."

"How do you know that?"

"The older ones already have their pecking order worked out. They don't argue, they just eat."

After several minutes passed, Jack whispered, "I can't go back to sleep."

"Just do it," Dad told him. "If you plan to ever be a scientist or an explorer, you've got to be able to tell your body what to do. Think *I have to sleep*, and you'll nod off in no time."

"Okay," Jack answered. "I'll give it a shot."

Dad turned away from him and went back to sleep. Jack pulled the sheets up to his shoulders, closed his eyes, and tried to will himself to sleep. But it was no use.

Memories of the day, combined with the anticipation of what they would do in the morning, kept his mind humming. They had arrived at the center at nightfall in a mud-caked truck that had tossed Jack around roughly all day. Wearing the brand-new bush shirt, cargo pants, and boots his mom had bought him, Jack sat between his father and a fellow scientist who drove the truck at top speed along a dirt road until it turned into tracks in the high grass. Jack could barely make out the tracks, but the driver followed them expertly. He was a young Tanzanian with long, straightened hair, wearing cargo pants, boots, and a leather jacket stamped with names of rock bands: the Rolling Stones, the Grateful Dead, the Police, Creedence Clearwater Revival. He looked like a rock musician himself, but Dad had introduced him as Bruce Gobukwe, a zoologist and pilot, and his coresearcher on the lion project. "How many lions have we tagged, Bruce?"

"Twenty and then some." Bruce laughed. His accent sounded British and his cheerful smile gave the impression he hadn't a care in the world. "Don't worry about the truck," he said, chuckling, after a bump that made Jack's head spin. "It's solid as a rock."

"You all right?" Dad patted his son's shoulder. "I threw up the first time I was on this road."

"I'm cool," Jack said between his teeth, trying his best to ignore the gymnastics in his stomach.

"Your son has nerves of steel, Alan." Then Bruce pointed. "Look—giraffes."

Jack counted five of them in the distance. When they heard the truck, the giraffes ran, but because their strides were so long, they appeared to move slowly. The sight took Jack's breath away.

Bruce popped in a CD and sang along with the Stones. On either side of the truck, the bluish mountains of western Tanzania loomed, savanna and scrub desert spreading across the valleys in between. Jack realized that he'd seen no signs of people for hours—no power lines, no villages, no other trucks on the road. Here and there, yellowish fog pulsed and flared above the grassland.

"Bushfires," Alan explained. "The heat out here makes the scrub kindle."

I'm so far from home, Jack thought, his head swimming with nausea and excitement at the same time. Both hands on the wheel, Bruce belted out the refrain to "Satisfaction" and glanced at Jack.

"We taking him lion tagging?" Bruce asked Dad.

Dad said something to Bruce in what could only be Swahili. Bruce answered in Swahili. *"Hatawa, hatawa."* He nodded, as if conceding a point. Jack had an English-Swahili dictionary in his Bergen shoulder sack that he'd paged through on the flight over, but he still couldn't understand what Dad had said.

"What are you guys talking about?"

"Our research. Sorry, we're used to mixing Swahili with English."

"What does *hatawa* mean?"

"It's the code name for our research project," Dad said. "Means 'action.' Not only action. It can also mean 'steps' and 'forward!' *Hatawa!* Forward!"

As the sun slipped behind a mountain, the

mud-coated truck pulled into the front yard of the research center. The center's buildings were large and built like colonial bungalows. Cars with doors and hubcaps missing were parked at random in the front yard. The place reeked of animals, mixed with the oily smoke from a crude kitchen. Two Tanzanian women were taking bedsheets off a clothesline. When Bruce cut the truck's engine, Jack could hear a generator humming quietly.

"Hey, Alan, you brought the cub!" Frank Aoyama called as he emerged from the cantina. Frank was a renowned professor and the center's senior scientist. He had known Jack since he was born. "Jesus, how much did you grow?"

Frank gave Jack a big hug. One of the consequences of Jack's parents' divorce was that Alan's friends no longer stopped by. When he was ten, Jack could boast that he knew scientists and bush pilots. Now he only had photos emailed from Africa to show his friends.

A few minutes later, a crowd of zoologists, anthropologists, and lab assistants gave Jack a tour of the compound. They showed him the labs, the dorm, the showers with open stalls, and the animal cages. There was also a fleet of paint-chipped single-engine planes. Jack's dad explained that the planes had been retrofitted to make them as weatherproof and durable as possible. With the limited funds their projects received, the research center couldn't afford to buy larger planes, so Dad and his colleagues were forced to make do with what they already had.

Jack looked around and took in his father's world. He saw a sign, chipped like the planes' paint: THE INTERNATIONAL CENTER FOR PRIMATOLOGY STUDIES. Dad led Jack and Bruce into the cantina for dinner.

"Smells like antelope steaks," Dad announced, turning to Jack. "Tomorrow morning Frank is going to show you how to date rocks. In the afternoon he's offered to take you fishing on Wasso Lake. How does that sound?"

Jack froze. "That wasn't the deal."

"The deal . . . " Dad echoed, trying to smile.

"The deal was you'd show me all your research. You yourself. Not Frank." Jack stared up at his dad. "I've seen you maybe two weeks in the last three years. Now I'm here and you're going to ditch me?"

"This way you can rest for a day or two, while I finish tagging lions," Dad replied. "I told your mom I'd break you in easy. Nothing dangerous. I promised. Tagging lions is routine research for me and Bruce, but if your mom hears about it—"

"But she's not here," Jack interrupted. "And I didn't fly nine thousand miles to be left behind."

After an awkward pause, Jack turned to Bruce. "How old were you when you first went out into the savanna alone?"

Bruce shrugged. "Nine. But I grew up here, in a village a few miles away. Kids had no choice but to go into the savanna alone. It was the only place we could get clean water."

Jack motioned toward his dad. "You didn't grow up here." He pointed through the cantina's open doorway, to a group of researchers gathered outside. "They didn't grow up here."

"Okay, okay," Dad said. The three of them sat down at a bare wooden table laid with army-style tin plates and cutlery. "You can come with us." Jack tried not to grin. "But we'll have to lay down some ground rules. You stay close to us at all times. And I guess it would help if you knew why we go out there in the first place. Lions are one of the most successful species around, top of the food chain. They're also highly socialized. I have a theory that when early humans moved onto the savanna, they learned many of their survival strategies from lions."

"Interesting," Jack said, paying close attention.

"As a species, lions are so different from us, but maybe early humans learned to eat meat by scavenging lion kills. And maybe the protein from the meat made a big developmental difference that helped their brains grow larger."

Jack looked at his dad with the eyes of an eager apprentice. "Seems like a valid theory," he said.

Bruce searched inside his jacket and pulled out a sturdy object with a button on one side. Bruce pressed it, and a blade with a serrated tongue and hooked end flashed out from the handle. The pilot set it on the table.

"An aardvark knife," he said. "A welcome present for you, Jack. If you plan to go rugged, you'll need some rugged gear."

Jack picked up the knife and looked it over. "Thanks." He smiled and shook Bruce's hand.

It was later that night that Jack awoke to the ter-
rifying sound of lions hunting. The aardvark lay
tucked in Jack's Bergen backpack, useless against
his fear of what stalked the night beyond the center's grounds.

CHAPTER TWO

At dawn the sun shot up above the horizon and light blasted onto the world all at once. Daylight poured into the army-style shower through a window grate. Despite lying awake for most of the night, Jack felt surprisingly alert when he left the dorm—full of still-sleeping researchers—and made his way to the shower house. Facing a scratched mirror, Jack combed his hands through his damp hair and noticed a note tacked next to the mirror: *Be a socialized primate—leave the place clean!* He smiled. As he opened the door to leave the shower house, he met a group of men carrying towels, toothbrushes, and shaving gear. "Up early, huh?" one of them greeted him.

"Right," Jack replied, heading toward the cantina. This morning the smell of cooking was homey and mouthwatering.

Earlier that morning, Jack had packed his Bergen with his new knife, a digital camera, a water bottle, two protein bars, his Swahili dictionary with a notepad and ballpoint pen attached, and a little tape recorder. In the cantina he set the bag on a table and took inventory of his supplies again. A Tanzanian woman in a flowered dress served him eggs and waffles.

"Your first trip into the savanna today?" she said, placing the plate in front of him.

Reaching for his knife and fork, Jack nodded.

"Eat up," she advised. "You're in for a long day."

Dad strolled in, eyes puffy and hair in disarray, and a few minutes later Bruce joined them.

After breakfast the three of them carried their gear to the airfield, where they stopped in front of the nose of the tiniest plane. They weighed themselves on industrial scales, then weighed their gear. Bruce and Dad loaded four extra drums of gasoline onto the plane; then they all climbed into the cockpit and fastened loose objects to the walls and floor. Jack wrapped the strap of his sack around a peg, and Dad clamped a bracket over it.

"Can't be too careful." Dad gave Jack a big smile, then sat down in the copilot's seat and put his headset on. Bruce sat in the pilot's seat reviewing a map.

Moments later, as the plane rolled down a runway of packed earth, Frank Aoyama sprang from the cantina and ran alongside the plane, yelling, "Have a great time! *Hatawa!*" Jack answered under his breath: *"Hatawa!"* Bruce fished out a tape from somewhere and pushed it into the tape deck. "Jumpin' Jack Flash" boomed in the cockpit as the little plane soared due west over the morning mist. Jack leaned back in his seat and told himself the adventure had begun.

For the next hour Jack gazed out the window, fascinated. The savanna felt so familiar already, perhaps because of the video postcards Dad had sent him over the last few years. The landscape was irregular: a patchwork of tall grass, tree clusters, and barren rocky hills. The plane passed over birds perched on the trees, and over herds of buffaloes and antelopes already grazing at this early hour. When the noisy plane's shadow swept over them, the herds startled and fled. The next cluster of rocks was covered with birds, and on the ground beneath them Jack spotted an ambling tribe of baboons.

The savanna appeared endless, and Jack realized it was much more vast than he had ever imagined. In the distance Jack could see the faint outline of the Witch's Pot, tall and green, capped by clouds at its peaks.

After that hour of gazing, Jack's sleepless night caught up with him. For a while he dozed, until a heavy thud against his chest jolted him awake. The plane was shaking so hard that the Bergen had flown from the peg and landed on his lap. His heart pounding, Jack elbowed the sack behind his seat. The cockpit was cast in twilight as the plane, creaking at every joint and seam, labored through violent storm clouds. But the rock music was still blaring, and his dad was calmly making notes on some papers spread on his knees.

Sensing that Jack was awake, he turned. "Don't worry—the plane's fine."

"But it's making so much noise," Jack said.

"It's like when you sit down and make a chair creak. It doesn't mean it will collapse under you. This is a Helio Courier, a good old American plane. It's a shame they stopped manufacturing them in the seventies."

This was little consolation to Jack, who just wished the shaking would stop. His body was still sore from the truck ride yesterday, and the plane's jerks only made it worse.

"What time is it, Dad?"

Dad glanced at his wristwatch. "Nine."

Jack did a quick calculation. They'd taken off at six A.M. Three hours of flying multiplied by a hundred knots—they were probably about three hundred thirty miles from the research center.

"Just hold on for a few more minutes," Dad said. He reached into a flight bag and pulled out a flight map, which was frayed along its edges from repeatedly being folded and unfolded. "This map's an old friend," he joked, turning his seat in order to face

Jack. He spread the map out, filling the space between them. "Look, here's the crater of the Witch's Pot." At first Jack couldn't identify the rim of the crater, because of the cryptic directional vectors and circles. Then he saw a very large circle, in the center of which was another circle. The outer circle was marked with dark-green shading.

"This is a double crater," Dad explained. "It's a hundred miles in diameter from outer rim to outer rim. We calculated the distance from satellite photos." On the map, the inside of the inner crater was unmarked by any terrain features. Dad tapped his finger on the blank area. "This second crater is still unexplored. The wind along the peaks is so strong, it wasn't until recently that we were able to fly over the outer rim. And that was only after we had this guy rebuilt." He affectionately stroked the aluminum wall of the cockpit.

Jack forgot about the plane's creaking. His attention was fixed on that uncharted inner crater.

"No one's been there, dad?"

"Not that I know of."

"What do you think is in there?"

"Grassland and some forest—we know that

from satellite photos. But we won't know much more than that until someone explores on the ground. This whole formation is a supervolcano. It's been dormant for the last four million years—at least that's what the geological analysis tells us. From what we can tell, two powerful eruptions created a crater within a crater—the Witch's Pot. When the primatology center can afford to buy a larger plane, we'll explore the inner crater. A small plane just can't handle the storms."

"There are always storms, every day?"

"Yes, because outside the volcano the air's cool and dry, but inside it's hot and humid, so storms form along the edge of the crater. They're worse on the inner rim. Now put your thumb here." He pointed to a spot on the map, next to the inner rim. Dad guided Jack's thumb across the inner crater, three thumb widths of space. "Your thumb's half an inch wide. At this map's scale that's about eighteen miles. So, straight across, the inner crater is at least fifty miles wide. There's a couple thousand square miles in there of what might be the most isolated terrain in Africa."

Dad refolded the map and placed it in the flight

bag. Suddenly the plane's propeller cut through ragged clouds and the sky appeared, a blinding blue. The shaking and bucking eased up. Jack looked out the window. Misty peaks fell back behind them. "And that was just the outer rim," Dad said.

Jack looked down, speechless.

The peaks were heavily forested, but as the plane descended, the grassland spread out before them. Animals were everywhere, and the grass and ponds and snaking little rivers glittered vividly. The sight below him was so intoxicating that Jack suddenly understood what had drawn his dad to Africa.

"Watch," Dad said, pushing a button on the instrument panel. The floor of the plane began to move. Jack cried out—the bottom of the plane was detaching!

A panel slid open, revealing a thick pane of glass fastened to the cockpit floor.

Peering through the floor as if it were a glass-bottomed boat, Jack saw a big herd beneath them: hundreds of wildebeests. Dust churned up by their hooves covered the glass, but the airflow wiped it clean again. Excited, he tapped his boots on the glass. "Can we open this?"

"Sure, when we start tagging!"

As if on cue, lions slid down from the rocks and cut in front of the herd. "Great! These guys are ideal for tagging," Dad yelled. He turned on the radar screen. "Most prides form around a pair of strong young males. After we tranquilize him from the plane, we go down and plant a chip—right here." Dad put his finger on the back of his neck. "The chip keeps track of the pride. Where they move, how often they hunt. And when the signal freezes, the tagged male will have fulfilled his duty as a pride leader. He'll be dead. But his offspring will keep forming new prides."

"Does the chip hurt?" Jack asked.

"Not a bit," Dad answered. "A tagged lion can hunt, crawl, swim, fight other males over territory or females. But his blip will always be here with me." Dad laughed, tapping his hand on the radar screen.

Jack nodded. Peeking between his boots, he saw a lion and several lionesses stand up on a rocky outcrop. As the plane zoomed by, Jack looked into the lion's eyes, staring up at the plane.

"We have enough gas to try to get that male?" Dad asked, unlatching a dart gun from the wall of the cockpit.

Bruce looked at his instruments. "We can stay in the air for another twenty minutes before I have to refuel. Go for it!"

Dad removed several darts from a box on the floor and loaded them into the magazine of the gun. He reached for a button to open the glass floor.

"Wait!" Jack stopped him. "Dad, can I try it?"

"I don't know, Jack," Dad replied. "This dart gun is heavier than it looks, and if you lost your balance . . . "

"I'm not going to lose my balance. And I carried all of Mom's old books up to the attic last week. Believe me, I can handle heavy things."

Bruce turned the plane for another pass over the lions.

Dad frowned. "This isn't a videogame, you know."

"Dad, I'm not a kid," Jack shouted. "I can *do* this."

Dad peered through the floor as the plane

approached the lions. "If your mother finds out . . ."

"She won't," Jack said firmly.

"Okay." Dad made sure the safety catch was on and relinquished the dart gun to Jack. "He's all yours."

The dart gun was not big—its barrel was shorter than Jack's arm from wrist to elbow—but Dad was right. It was heavy.

"Listen," Dad said, "if you need to take a break, don't point the gun inside the cockpit. One dart in Bruce, and he'll keel over in two seconds flat. What do you weigh, Bruce?"

"One-ninety," Bruce replied.

"Right. Lions can weigh up to six hundred pounds, so that dart packs a mighty punch. You put Bruce to sleep while he's at the controls, I don't want to have to jump in and take over. You sure you don't want to let me try first?"

"No, no. I'll do it," Jack replied, gripping the gun tightly.

Dad pushed a button. The glass floor slid open, and cold air rushed in.

"Now be patient," Dad yelled above the noise. "Wait till Bruce lowers the plane right above him."

"Uh-huh." Jack felt sweat on his upper lip. He licked it away quickly.

The herd stampeded under the plane, and Jack struggled to see through the cloud of dust stirred up by a flurry of hooves. The wildebeests' brown humps merged into a river of hooves and horns as the lions approached. Jack moved down to lie flat on his belly at the edge of the opening and held the dart gun to his side.

"There he is!" Dad urged, pointing at the male, who was standing to one side of the herd. "Go for it!" Jack raised the dart gun and tried to take aim, but the lion was so obscured by dust, he couldn't keep the sight on him.

"Move your eyes with the herd," Dad instructed. That was good advice: Jack's eyes found the lion— still crouching on one side of the herd. The two lionesses joined him and dove ahead, scattering the running wildebeests. The male, inexperienced and disturbed by the noise of the plane, hesitated. "Squint," Dad yelled over the rushing wind. "It'll help your aim!"

The slipstream made Jack's eyes burn. He took aim and pulled the trigger. The trigger didn't move.

"The safety catch!" Dad yelled.

Jack reached to release it. As he did, a swath of dust swept up from beneath the plane and pelted his arms and face. Jack pulled back from the hatch, coughing violently.

"Get up!" Dad yelled, pulling Jack up by his shoulders. Bruce punched a button and the hatch closed. Dad opened the cockpit's side window. "Shoot from here," he said, guiding the gun in Jack's hands. "Bruce, turn!"

The plane turned as Jack spotted the three lions in the midst of the fleeing herd. One female clumsily clawed a wildebeest's nose as the other lioness sank her teeth into its rump.

"First timers!" Dad chuckled. *Like me,* Jack thought, angry at himself for forgetting about the safety catch.

Weighed down by lionesses, the wildebeest couldn't move. The male paced around, undecided. Jack tried to get the male in his sights, but it was hard. The plane moved, the lion moved. Jack fired. The lion's tail twitched as if to swat a mosquito.

"Missed! Again!" Dad ordered.

Jack fired again.

The male leaped on top of the wildebeest with the females, and the whole pile collapsed. But the wildebeest, bleeding from its mouth and hindquarters, managed to shake off the predators and darted away. The lion staggered up. Confused, he reared on his hind legs, roaring at the plane's passing shadow.

"Now!" Dad yelled. "He's not moving!"

Jack shot at the lion again. And again.

A little spot of blood appeared on the lion's rump.

"I got him!" Jack cried.

"He'll be down any second," Dad yelled. Jack watched the male sink into the tall grass. "Bingo!"

The females ran off toward a boulder, their muscles rolling under their tawny fur. As Bruce brought the plane down, the engine sputtered, but he nosed it up with the last few ounces of fuel, and they landed as the engine cut out.

=╫=

THEY CLIMBED OUT of the plane and walked abreast, Jack with the reloaded dart gun strapped to his shoulder.

"I can't believe I shot a dart right into a lion!" Jack exclaimed. "Where do you think he is, Dad?"

27

"He's around here somewhere," Dad said, smiling at Jack's excitement. He had filled his arms with a lunch basket and had a six-pack of Cokes balanced under his chin.

Walking on Jack's other side, Bruce smiled too. His leather bag was packed with plastic containers filled with labeled caps, surgical gloves, a Polaroid, a digital camera, and shiny little objects that looked like pens: the chips. The batteries inside would last up to twenty years.

As Bruce and Dad stepped through the grass, they lifted their boots high and brought them down with a thud. They pounded out their steps, advertising their presence to snakes and other hidden creatures. First rule of survival in the bush: Don't get stung by something you can't see. It was the first thing Dad had taught Jack when they'd arrived at the center.

The lion's fawn-colored body appeared in the grass so unexpectedly, Jack gasped. Mosquitoes buzzed over the lion's mouth and hindquarters. Jack tried to take it all in: the dusty fur, the huge carnassial teeth, the massive paws. Then the lion twitched, and the mosquitoes scattered. The lion staggered up, his droopy eyes level with Jack's face.

Jack saw his father and Bruce freeze—but he kept walking toward the animal, carried by his own momentum before he could register what was happening. He took the gun from his shoulder, aimed, and pulled the trigger. It was jammed.

His father dropped the lunch basket and raised his hand, gesturing that the safety catch was still on. In a panic, Jack pulled it back. He didn't even aim, just fired the dart. It shot into the lion's chest, about two inches under the frilled edge of the mane. The lion tried to leap but then collapsed, his eyes glazed.

Stunned, Jack was still aiming the gun when Dad caught up to him and yanked him away from the lion. Dad nudged the lion's motionless belly with his foot. The lion uttered a sleepy complaint.

"He's out, Jack," Dad reassured him. "I don't think we'll have another surprise like that today."

Bruce opened the leather bag. Dad reached in and pulled out a chip. He plunged it into the lion's thick neck like a medical syringe and stepped back. As if breaking a spell, he gestured to Jack for the dart gun. Jack shook off his shock and handed it over.

"One shot," Dad muttered. "If you were hunting with a spear, that's all you would have. One shot."

"You have good reflexes, Jack," Bruce said. He walked around the body, knelt down beside it, and called out: "Here's where you got him from the plane!"

Jack ran to the spot. He saw a little gash where a spurt of blood had dried behind the shoulder, near the spine.

Jack nudged the lion with his boot. "Is he okay with two darts in him?"

"Oh, he'll be fine." Dad measured the body with his eyes. "He's much bigger than he looked from the plane. Seven hundred pounds at least. Come here, Jack." Dad lifted one of the lion's front paws. "Hold this, feel how heavy it is!" Jack took a breath and grabbed the paw. It was soft, but the tendons and bones within it felt as hard as cables.

"How much does it weigh?" he stammered.

"About twenty pounds, claws to wrist."

Jack let the tawny leg fall to the ground.

Bruce got out a measuring tape and a Polaroid camera. He measured the male from head to tail and punched notes into his laptop. Dad scratched his forehead under the brim of his bush hat. "Jack, do you want to take some pictures of him up close?"

"Sure." Jack pulled his digital camera out of the Bergen. He moved back to take a wide shot. Bruce had set up his laptop on the ground, right by the hind paws. He clacked the keys, inserting data about the new tag.

Dad set the lunch basket on the grass and opened it. "Let's eat," he called.

"In a minute," Jack said, still walking backward to get a good shot.

Behind him there was only a spread of flat, bare rock. There was no grass, no vegetation at all to give a crouching animal cover. Very safe. From the rock he got a shot of the lion, Dad, and Bruce all together, with the plane in the background. Walking back, Jack tripped on a pebble and stumbled. He looked down. Under his boots, the flat rock was dry and old like a moonscape.

Then he saw them: footprints!

CHAPTER THREE

They looked more like hands than feet. The prints were narrow, and the toes were long, like fingers. Only the big toes looked human at all, thick and splayed out. There were six prints in a trail heading toward the outer rim.

Standing up, Jack faced the inner rim and remembered seeing it on the map. A round crenellation of crests, it looked taller than the rim they had already flown over. The peaks churned with storm clouds, even darker and more ominous than those on the outer rim. Jack concluded that if something had survived the journey over them, it must have happened thousands of years earlier, before the rim was fully formed.

He jumped up and yelled to Dad and Bruce, who sprinted over as if Jack were in immediate danger. Dad saw the little trail and looked at Jack, dumbstruck. He got down on his knees, careful not to disturb the prints, and gently placed his hand over one of them.

Dad's palm covered the print completely. He carefully probed it with his fingers.

"You can touch this, Jack," he said softly. "It won't crumble. It's really old."

Jack knelt beside him and placed his palm on top of the print. The indentation felt hardened and dry, like an old bone. Jack shivered. If the footprints were *really* old, he knew what that could mean. He was not Alan Conran's son for nothing. Well-preserved evidence of early human's presence millions of years ago was as rare as it was highly prized by the scientific community. Footprints like this at Laetoli, another Tanzanian research site, had brought their discoverers fame and fortune.

"The first hunter-gatherers had to walk for

hours each day to find food. In the process they left footprints, most of which disappeared, obviously." Dad's eyes shone as he spoke excitedly. "But there are a few places in the world—very few, Jack—where their footprints have been so well preserved. Some are in what would have been muddy swamps, but these were made in volcanic ash that cooled after an eruption and eventually hardened. Like this."

"How old are they?" Jack asked.

His father shook his head. "I can't give you an exact age without dating them, but they're old. Really old."

"They're from primates, though, right?"

"Apes walk like this," Dad said, standing. He spread his legs and lumbered forward with his feet apart and his knees bent. He waddled slowly for a few steps and stopped. "Humans are the only mammals in the world who walk with a real two-legged stride. Whoever made these prints balanced their weight on one foot, then switched to the other in an unbroken stride. That's a real bipedal walk—apes can't do it. When apes walk on two legs, they sway from side to side because their knees can't straighten completely, so after a few steps, they go back to walking on all fours. A sustained bipedal stride is a uniquely human trait." He turned abruptly to Bruce. "The team needs to see this. We need to make a positional record. Is there paint in the plane?"

Bruce ran over and retrieved a canister of spray paint from the cockpit.

Dad took the can and walked a wide circle around the prints, spraying a red line on the ground while Jack busily documented the site with his digital camera. Jack was thrilled to be included in this discovery. He truly felt like he was part of the team. As Bruce was setting up a tripod, they heard a muffled moan.

"Damn," Bruce said. "The lion."

"Where's the gun?" Jack asked.

"Back there. Let's hope he's still groggy."

Dad dropped the spray paint and ran to where the tagged lion was staggering to his feet, drooling. "Go on!" Dad urged the animal, waving his arms. He and Bruce ran circles around him, yelling "Go! Go!"

Hearing their yells, the two lionesses bolted forth from the grass, and as Dad and Bruce fell back, the females loped to their dazed pride leader and licked his face. When the trio trotted off into the savanna, Dad's attention returned to the footprints.

"We need to get up in the air and take some shots from above." Dad frowned, staring into the expanse of tall grass. The sky was turning dark as storm clouds moved toward them over the rim of the inner crater.

"I agree, Alan," Bruce said. "But it looks like there's a front coming this way."

"This crater is thousands of square miles," Dad persisted. "What if we can't find our way back here?"

Jack looked at his dad, whose face was taut with anxiety. If they lost track of those prints, Jack realized, his father would be devastated.

Suddenly it started to pour. The group grabbed their gear and ran to the plane. The fuselage didn't give them enough cover from the wind, so Bruce pulled out a tarp and raised it on four stakes he carried in the plane.

"Listen," Bruce said. "Even if I could get the plane up in this weather, we wouldn't get a clear shot of the site with all the rain."

"Then we'll wait it out," Dad declared.

Dad, Jack, and Bruce sat under the tarp and ate sandwiches, waiting for the storm to pass. Although the winds were still too high for flying, the rain stopped at nightfall, so Bruce pulled the sides of the tarp down to form a tent.

Dad, eager to return to the footprints, searched inside the plane and emerged with two giant flashlights, South African Bush Blasters. "Want to take another look at that trail, Jack?" Jack was ready. He grabbed a Blaster and turned it on, sending a fat beam of light across the wet grass ahead. Dad called to him to walk making as much noise as he could, even though the flashlights were bright enough to ward off predators. They came to the footprints and shone the lights on them.

"I can't believe this," Dad said suddenly. Jack's hair pricked up. The trail was much longer than they'd been able to see earlier. Alan followed it with the Blaster's beam. It stretched several yards in the direction of the outer rim.

Jack could feel his heart pounding. Dad ran to the end of the trail, lunged to the ground, and put his palms on the prints. He stood up, blinking in the beam of Jack's Blaster, and motioned for him to take a look. Jack ran to his side, crouched down, and examined the ground. These prints were shallower, but just as hardened as the others, cradling puddles of rainwater.

Dad got up. He experimented with the beam of the flashlight, holding it some two feet from the ground, shining it laterally onto the prints. Then he said, "These are more eroded. They may be even older than the others. If they hadn't filled with rain, we might not have seen them at all." He showed Jack how the beam shone on the few ounces of water in each indent. "I think what we're looking at is some kind of ancient hunting path. As the early humans who lived inside this crater grew in numbers, they may have exhausted the resources around them, so they looked for new hunting ground, beyond the Witch's Pot." He tousled Jack's hair. "Maybe you have the gift, Jack, the gift of discovery. If you hadn't spotted these, it might have been another hundred years before someone discovered them."

Jack was breathless. The idea of early bipedal

creatures treading the same ground where he stood now with Dad was mind-blowing.

"But how could they live in the crater," Jack said, "if the volcano was active?"

Dad laughed quietly. "They probably settled here after the volcano had already become dormant, when the savanna had grown up in the crater. I imagine this would have been a pretty isolated environment even then. Too bad they left. I bet this was a treasure trove of evolutionary diversity." Dad swept the Blaster around. A bird took off, but otherwise the place was empty. "Sit down, Jack—it's safe," he said.

They sat next to each other on the petrified ash.

"This is an incredible find, Jack. There's no limit to what we could understand about evolution by studying a place like this. If early humans developed in isolation here, other species probably did too. It will take a lot of hard work to prove that, but by the time you go to college, this might be another Olduvai Gorge." He paused. "If I get the funding to dig it. But with evidence like this"—he gestured at a footprint—"I'm sure I'll get the money."

"How long will that take, Dad?"

"If I get the grants, five years. Maybe even longer." He turned to his son as if he'd just remembered something. "God, you must be exhausted. This has been quite a day."

Jack didn't reply. The thought of his father being away from home for another five years made him forget about the time.

On the ground he saw a little round stone, darker than the gray bed of ash. Jack picked it up, feeling how snugly it fit in his fist. He tucked it into a side pocket. Something to remember this night by.

=╫=

WHEN THEY RETURNED to the makeshift tent, Jack was so tired that he slept deeply, despite the hardness of the ground and the wind rattling the tarp. He awoke to his father shaking him. "Quick, there's a break in the weather!"

Bruce had refueled and was already revving up the plane.

The dawn was cold and gray, and the wind was blowing hard from the outer rim.

They picked up their sleeping bags and the tarp and ran to the plane. Jack dashed back for his Bergen, then jumped into the cockpit as Dad

40

slammed the hatch shut. They strapped on their seat belts, and Bruce sped the plane down the grassland until they took off.

"Jack, help me out," Dad said. He heaped their three cameras into Jack's lap, then opened the floor panel to take photos through the glass. The sky was clear, but the plane creaked in the wind.

"Pass me the digital," Dad yelled over the wind. "And count how many shots we take—we have only so much memory on the card." Jack handed Dad his digital and tucked the other two cameras in the flight bag. Dad instructed Bruce to fly lower and slower. Bruce tried to find a smooth flying ceiling so Dad could get some good shots.

"I'm sorry," Bruce said, gripping the joystick with both hands. "The wind has shifted. It's much stronger than yesterday, and it's pushing us into the crater."

"We can't lose those prints, Bruce!" Dad yelled. "Whatever you can do!"

Concentrating intensely, Bruce maneuvered the plane closer to the site, but as they approached, the plane careened toward the peaks of the inner rim. The wind moving over them buffeted the plane from all sides, making it rock and sway through the air.

"The witch." Bruce didn't sound amused.

He probed the peaks, flying toward them, then turning several times. Dad handed the camera back to Jack. "Put it away for now. It's too rough out there."

Jack slipped the camera back into the Bergen, the strap of which he had wrapped around his wrist to secure it. The Helio's wings shook in the gusts.

"More prints! There!" Dad pointed toward a string of what looked like tiny narrow cups along the ground. *"Hatawa!"* he exclaimed excitedly, like a hunter amazed by an abundance of prey. Bruce looked down, smiled, and mouthed the same word. *"Hatawa!"* There was more than one trail down there—there were many trails!

"How old?" Jack shouted.

But Dad was busy talking to Bruce, who was trying to turn into the wind.

"The plane doesn't have enough power," Bruce yelled. "We have to turn back!" Dust lashed at the windshield and the craft shook.

"All right, let's get out of here." Dad nodded.

"We can find the site again—we'll come back with a bigger plane." He looked intently at his son. "Jack, don't worry. We'll be back."

"You're on," Jack said. Just then, the plane bucked as though it had struck something solid.

Jack heard the windshield crack.

Suddenly Bruce's seat belt gave and he was hurled into the controls. His head lolled back as if his neck were broken. Jack's father lunged to the panel, but the plane tumbled toward the peaks of the inner rim. Rocky crags punched at the glass under Jack's feet, which shattered. The luggage rack above Jack sprang from its mountings, sending their bags flying.

At the controls, Dad was trying to fight the wind, but the plane was being sucked over the rim into the inner crater. Dad fought to keep the plane above the treetops, until one of them ripped a hole in the floor, slashing past Jack's feet.

Jack threw up.

The plane slammed onto a rock ledge. The fuselage cracked, and Jack, still seated and belted in, was thrown from the plane.

As JACK FELL through the trees, the seat came apart and the belt broke. He tore through an acacia tree and felt searing pain in his right arm. His clothes snagged in the branches, slowing his descent, while up on the ledge the plane burst into flames. Jack's feet touched the ground as a creature bolted from the bushes and lobbed a rock at his face. Jack blacked out.

THE CREATURE that had thrown the stone was poised to throw again. But the body that had fallen from the sky lay still. Just then, another object tumbled from the acacia's branches and struck the ground beside the body. A shiny thing spilled out of the bag, buzzing, clicking, over and over. The creature slammed its heel against it, silencing the camera forever.

PART 2

WITCH'S POT, WESTERN TANZANIA

CHAPTER ONE

Jack blinked in darkness. He felt around, touching ground. Soil rained over his face and chest; he stopped moving, terrified. The air smelled earthy, dank.

Where am I? Jack thought, fighting the impulse to panic. He stretched his legs and felt around with his boots and knees.

He was alive. Fear indicated life.

Pain pulsed through his body. He was cut everywhere—on his chest, the back of his neck, his shoulders, and his legs. His right arm, caked in mud above his elbow, felt wrapped in a hot band of pain. Was it broken?

He tried to part his lips, to call for help, but they were so scraped and swollen, he could barely open them. Each breath was painful. He slurred: "Da-ad?" He tried to call louder. "Dad? Bruce? Where are you?"

Above him, lions roared menacingly.

He listened with desperate attention. They seemed so close, rough and real. Until yesterday—was it yesterday?—the plane, and Dad and Bruce, had insulated him from danger. Now danger surrounded him. A hungry feline could reach in here anytime. Or the dirt walls around him might collapse, filling his nostrils, choking him to death. The fear of being buried alive was worse than that of being attacked by lions. Jack bolted up. His head struck a soft ceiling of soil. He was in a burrow of some kind, hopefully in the tall grass, hidden from predators.

Jack smelled burning rubber—the plane's tires. *Since the plane didn't explode on impact,* Jack thought hopefully, *Dad and Bruce might still be alive.*

But then fear washed over him again. When the

tires finished burning, would the lions be able to smell him? He stroked his swollen, painful arm, gritting his teeth. The blood and earth had mixed together, forming a kind of natural bandage over the wound. He wasn't bleeding now, but he felt feverish, and so thirsty.

Pain, thirst, and fear made it hard for Jack to think straight. He used his uninjured hand to pull himself up out of the burrow. He noticed that the stars above the grass were fading, and he hoped dawn was on its way. As he lifted his shoulders above the hole, he saw something that looked like a severed head. Jack screamed, swinging his good hand toward the shape, but when he did, he fell back into the burrow.

He sat in the burrow for a moment, summoning his courage. He had to get out of there, severed head or no. Once again he pulled himself up out of the hole, this time taking a closer look at the fearful thing.

It was a kind of gourd, like a large papaya, a split in one side glistening in the starlight.

He picked it up, and its juice ran down his fingers. It was pulpy and tasted sweet when he licked it. He dug his fingers into the split, but he couldn't break the fruit in two. Sitting in the burrow, fruit in his hands, he tried to make a plan for the next few hours. Dawn was on its way. At dawn he would pull himself out of the burrow, walk through the tall grass into the open, and call for help. If his father or Bruce could hear him, they'd answer. Calling out would give him away to predators, but he had no choice. If he spotted danger, he'd run back to the burrow. Many animals built sophisticated lairs, with tunnellike passages and more than one exit. Maybe this was one of them. Jack yelled into the darkness of the hole, trying to gauge its depth. Something in the way the earth carried his voice gave him the feeling that he was no longer alone in the burrow. He was certain, in fact, that something was right next to him—skin to skin! Eyes glowed in the darkness. Horrified, Jack struck wildly toward them and felt beside him a tough, muscular body. He landed a punch, knocking the thing on its back, but it hurled its feet at Jack's face. Everything went dark.

JACK COULD HEAR birds singing. *Some of those birds will be eaten by predators in the next few hours,* he thought with strange detachment. *Just like that. Everything can become prey out here. Where's my knife? I fell out of the plane with the Bergen strapped to my wrist—it should be close by. Maybe the knife's still in it. I need the knife, in case that creature returns.*

There was some feeble light now. Dawn was coming. Jack peered around and saw that the burrow stretched into a tunnel, gray with daylight. He lifted himself up to the opening again. Beyond the tall grass, on a rocky ledge, the plane was still smoldering.

I'm not far from the crash site, Jack thought, *but how did I get here? I don't remember walking or crawling. Was I dragged here?* He thought of the creature and remembered the force of its feet. *It had to be an ape*, he thought. *It had ape feet. But why did it help me?*

He'd never heard of apes or monkeys burrowing under the ground.

At any rate, whatever had dragged him down here had kept him from becoming a meal for the lions. For now.

So, what next? he wondered as he settled back

into the burrow. *I have to get out of here. I'll conserve my energy and try to think straight.* Something dark filled up the burrow entrance, blocking the daylight. An animal was crawling toward him. Jack panicked. He shouted, "Dad . . . Bruce! Help!"

On all fours, daylight silhouetting its body, the creature paused momentarily, then advanced. Jack freed his injured arm and frantically searched his clothes, desperate to find a weapon. Nothing. He stared, terrified, as the creature came closer. It had wispy hair that stood straight up from its sloped forehead. Its nostrils were two palpitating little holes, and its eyes were right under its hairline.

An ape, Jack reassured himself, as the gray light revealed the creature. *A small male ape.*

The ape advanced, and then a chimplike hand held out a large green leaf with water cupped in it. The ape poured some of the water onto the ground, where it pooled in the dirt.

"Thank you," Jack rasped.

The ape reached inside his armpit and took out a stone. Then, with his long-fingered hand, he held it as if ready to throw it. And then Jack saw the fear in the ape's eyes.

He's afraid of me, as I'm afraid of him.

And then, still rational despite being terrified, Jack crawled forward, head low like an animal, conceding submission. He dipped his face in the water before it all seeped into the ground. Drinking in this position, Jack showed the ape he was totally vulnerable. The ape inched forward and poured a few more drops of water into the little puddle. Jack lapped at the water until it was gone.

When he lifted his head, the ape sidled away from him, the palms of his feet pale in the faint light of the cave.

Jack sat down, his lips muddied. *It's not a dream.* Instead of pinching his arm, he bit his lip, which was swollen and painful. *No, definitely not a dream.*

He pressed his dirty hand to his face. The skin was hot to the touch. *I have to get my temperature down,* Jack thought.

Daylight was blazing now through the opening of the burrow. The ape returned with a broken branch, which he soldered to Jack's arm by packing mud around it. Jack's skin tickled through the searing pain in his arm. The branch was covered with bugs. Next to him, the ape crouched and those high-set eyes blinked. He started to crush the bugs on Jack's arm, mashing them into his open flesh. The gash grew numb. The ape spat what looked like white squiggles onto Jack's arm. Larvae? As one foot held Jack down, the ape pressed the larvae into the wound with his mouth. Jack didn't fight. He watched, amazed. He felt like he was sleeping through it all, wide-eyed.

The guys at the center will send a rescue plane, he thought, trying to absorb the shock of his situation. *I've got to get to a place where they can see me, and stand up and signal to it when it comes.* Then he remembered the storms churning above the rim. Would a rescue plane be able to make it through?

Discouraged and exhausted, he slumped to one side, watching the ape tend to his arm. At least he wasn't alone.

CHAPTER TWO

When he woke again, Jack realized he had lost track of time.

A gray, rainy dawn greeted him when he crawled out of the burrow, finally stood aboveground, stepped out of his boots, and peeled off his mud-caked clothes. Naked, he wiped the mud off his body as raindrops bathed his face. He opened his mouth and drank from the sky, then pulled his boots back on. The bandage of mud and insects hadn't washed off the gash on his upper arm. Staring closely, he saw large red ants:

Mandibles exposed, they had been kneaded into the mud on his arm. *Like stitches!* Jack thought. Larvae, fat and white, flecked the mud too. He whipped around—the ape sat two steps away with a large leaf covering his head like an umbrella.

Jack stared at him, stupefied. No longer in the twilight of the burrow, the ape looked like none Jack had ever seen before. His face sloped toward a dark-lipped mouth, and his teeth were tinted green from chewing leaves. His arms curled with muscles and his legs were strong and sturdy. There was downy growth on his groin, but the rest of his body was hairless. His feet were narrower than a chimpanzee's, and his toes were long and finger-like. The ape's body was scarred everywhere, but all the scars looked long healed.

Jack saw his soaked Bergen lying on the grass nearby. The little ape had broken the Bergen's zipper, or it had broken in the fall. Next to the bag lay a water bottle, uncapped and almost empty, a PowerBar crawling with ants, and Jack's digital camera, which was bashed in so badly, the lens was completely gone.

The rain stopped, and the ape took off the leaf

as if it were a hat, threw it aside, and stood up. Now that he was standing full height, Jack guessed the creature was barely four feet tall.

How old is he? Jack wondered, recalling what he knew about primates. *Ten, maybe?* They generally looked older than humans of comparable age, because their faces were more wrinkled. Sometimes chimp babies looked bafflingly old. But the little ape had no wrinkles, except for one where his forehead met his bristling hair. The wrinkle stretched almost all the way across his forehead. *He's a kid,* Jack decided, less frightened now. *But what kind of ape kid makes bandages out of ants and mud?*

"Where are your folks?" Jack mumbled aloud, not sure if talking was a good idea, since he might scare the ape, or make him respond aggressively.

"Eeee," the ape answered, staring at Jack with concentration.

Apes spoke too, Jack remembered, in "ape thirty-six," as his dad called the higher primates' basic thirty-six sounds. Each of those sounds carried a different meaning: *I've found food, I smell a predator, I'm scared.* The ape had just given Jack an answer. With a foot that looked like a hand, he pushed the camera, the PowerBar, and the water bottle next to each other, almost in a straight line. Then he pulled two stones from his armpits and set them on the ground next to Jack's possessions, and as dazed as he was, Jack almost laughed. He nodded, acknowledging the gift: "Right, I needed some of those. Good thinking . . . Stone Boy."

The ape looked at Jack's shirt and pants, lying on the wet grass like shed snakeskins. Jack reached for his pants. Stone Boy growled sharply. Jack froze. In a quick glance, the ape's eyes moved from Jack's boots, to Jack's legs, his body, and finally his face. *You're different!* his quizzical look signaled to Jack.

"You think *I'm* strange," he mumbled. "What kind of weirdo runs around with rocks in his armpits?" As if ending the conversation, the ape picked up his stones and disappeared into the tall grass.

Jack pulled on his soaked shirt and cargo pants, which were heavy from the rain. He wiped the PowerBar on his shirt and ate it in two quick bites. The sugar went right to his head, and he immediately felt dizzy. He'd packed two PowerBars in his sack. If he could find the other one, he'd save it for the next day. The rescue plane might not arrive until tomorrow, or even the day after. He picked up the Bergen, poured the mud out of it, and retrieved the aardvark knife, which was still inside. Stone Boy had missed the knife. Jack threw it back in the sack, and the plastic bottle too, thinking it might come in handy. Now he would find Dad and Bruce. He found a bush with large leaves weighted down by rain, slurped water out of them until he'd quenched his thirst, and streaked ahead through the tall grass.

Wind parted the grass. Dead ahead, Stone Boy sat still, his attention fixed. He had found Jack's English-Swahili dictionary and was cracking it open. The wind flipped through its pages. Stone Boy jerked, and his shoulders shook in surprise as if the book were a live creature. The pages whipped back and forth until the ape slapped the book shut again. He stroked the shiny cover with his thick thumb and rubbed its smoothness on his chin.

He's never seen a book. And he's afraid of it! Jack

marveled. *But he's so curious. . . .*

Jack looked past him and saw the downed plane on a rock ledge some fifty feet above the savanna. From this distance he could see that its wings were broken, and its nose and tail were missing entirely.

Jack wanted more than anything to see his father stand up on those rocks and wave at him. If Dad was not by the plane, maybe he had made it to the rim and was trying to hike out for help. Jack decided to check out the plane and headed for the rocks.

A few yards from Stone Boy, tall whistling thorns rustled. A lion crawled out of them, his mane crumpled and paws muddy. The lion's gaze moved from Jack to the ape and back to Jack.

Jack wanted to yell a warning, but the ape had already looked up. The lion stepped toward Stone Boy, who dropped the book and dove behind an acacia tree. Jack felt his pockets. Empty. He remembered the feel of the dart gun in his hands, and Dad saying "One shot." He thrust his fist inside his sack and grabbed the aardvark. But its blade was so tiny, it would be useless against a lion. One shot. *"Haaaahhh!"* Jack yelled, raising his arms high above his head.

The lion paused before advancing with small steps, shoulders low to the ground.

Jack had read that human odors made lions nervous—maybe the smell of sweat would frighten the animal off. Jack peeled off his shirt and threw it toward the lion. The lion sniffed it and sat back on his hind legs as though confused. At that moment, wiry fingers grabbed Jack's hand and pulled him toward the rocks. Another lion, older looking, appeared behind the first one, and they greeted each other with muted roars. They leaped toward Jack and Stone Boy, who zigzagged, changing course several times as they ran toward the rocks. Jack gasped, but not in fear.

"What the . . . ?" The little ape in front of him was running as fast as he could, but not like an ape at all. Stone Boy was nearly upright, lifting his knees almost to his chest. Jack couldn't believe his eyes. How was it possible?

Just then Stone Boy lunged at a baboon foraging on the cliff face, smacking him hard. The baboon screeched, and suddenly, out of clefts and holes in the rocks, a troop appeared. When they saw the lions, the baboons bared their teeth and hurled dirt at the felines, stopping them in their tracks. The lions' playtime was over.

Stone Boy hauled Jack onto the rocks. Safely out of the lions' range, he broke into a chattering howl of pure relief. Then he turned to Jack and screeched at him as if to say, *Don't ever back down, not even before a lion!* Jack laughed nervously in response, slowly realizing that he had just truly faced death for the first time. And, he realized, he'd done it with a companion who might be more boy than ape after all.

CHAPTER THREE

J ack and Stone Boy lay on the rock ledge, their chests heaving. The baboon troop regrouped below, plopped down on their rears, and groomed one another. The nearness of the two bipeds didn't seem to bother them.

Stone Boy sat up, staring at Jack's skin, which had quickly turned raw and red in the unforgiving sun. He touched Jack's shoulder with his index finger, picked up one dusty booted foot and then the other. Jack tried to sit still as Stone Boy bobbed around him. Unaware of his own nakedness, Stone

Boy ran his hand over the stitched cuffs of the cargo pants, then pulled the pockets inside out. He stood on a rock and touched Jack's filthy hair, which was now stiff with dust just like his own. He raised his shoulders in a shrug, as if to say: However strange you are, you *are*. He touched Jack with his feet as often as with his hands. Jack's mind rambled: *Those feet like a chimp's: they grip the rock so well, but they can run too. So why would ape feet change into human feet? The way ape feet are shaped is one of evolution's successes!* Upon closer inspection, Jack realized, Stone Boy's footprints looked just like the ones he'd found outside the inner rim with his dad and Bruce. Jack's jaw dropped. Suddenly he understood his father's quest, his obsession, against all odds, to understand the unknown. A piece of that unknown, alive and real, had saved Jack's life.

Dad's lifetime of research, even the discovery of the footprints, was nothing compared to the thrill of being in the company of a living fossil. But the way he ran, the shape of his face, the hairless body—Stone Boy didn't quite fit the description of any hominid fossil species Jack had ever studied.

Even the brilliant Alan Conran could not have imagined Stone Boy as he had revealed himself to Jack. Whatever species Stone Boy represented, as far as Jack could tell, had to be a cousin whose ancestors had branched off nearly at the end of human evolution's journey from ancient primate to modern man. Perhaps Stone Boy was descended from a missing link scientists didn't know was missing. A link Dad hadn't known was missing.

Be alive, Dad, Jack hoped silently. *Be alive, so you can see him.*

Lost in his thoughts, Jack suddenly realized that Stone Boy had disappeared. But before he could panic, the little ape reappeared holding a tiny animal. It looked like a squirrel, but Jack couldn't be sure, because Stone Boy had smashed it against a rock. He bit off the head and held up the body to Jack, inviting him to share. Jack shook his head and turned away. Stone Boy stuffed the rest of the squirrel in his mouth and kicked the leftovers into the slender African horsetails that filled the spaces between rocks. *Smart choice*, Jack thought, looking at the plant. *It's not easy for herbivores to get up here and eat you.* Stone Boy washed the squirrel down with a slurp of rainwater from a crack in the rock. Jack dipped his mouth in another crack, getting a mouthful of water and dust and tiny drowned bugs. But he forced himself to drink it. Could he eat raw meat? Maybe, when his hunger overcame his initial revulsion. He looked at the inner rim where the plane had crossed over before crashing. Always, storm clouds swirled above the peaks.

"Frank has to know where I am," Jack said under his breath. Frank would send a rescue plane with paramedics and bush trackers, a plane big enough to make it over the inner rim. All Jack had to do was survive a few days and keep himself sane. The plan, for now, was to find Dad, who was looking for him too, Jack assured himself. Had Jack not been in the burrow for a few days, Dad probably would have found him already.

Jack and Stone Boy started toward the plane, but they had gone only a few steps when they encountered the stench of burned matter and a cloud of biting flies. Jack slapped his chest and neck, but it was no use. A gust of wind finally swept the flies away. Jack called out to Stone Boy: "Come on! *Ndege!*" Bruce had told him that *ndege* meant

"airplane" in Swahili. "Come on! *Ndege! Hatawa!*"
Stone Boy ran to catch up.

There was a screeching noise ahead, harsh, scraping. The plane was moving. Jack's heart started pounding. They rounded a tall bush and saw the plane's detached rudder, embedded like a giant axe in the rock. A piece of paper picked up by the breeze was drifting quickly past them—Jack lunged so abruptly, he knocked Stone Boy over the edge of the rock. Jack stopped in his tracks and peered over the edge. Stone Boy was already scrambling up.

"Come on," Jack urged him impatiently. Jack ran to the paper and picked it up, realizing instantly it was a piece of the flight map. He turned it over in his fingers with a strange feeling that his father had placed it on the ground for him to discover. As he pulled himself up the rock face, Jack spotted Stone Boy ahead, staring at what lay on the ledge. When Jack caught up, he saw what used to be the plane's cockpit and a flurry of birds on top of it. Jack ran toward the wreckage, waving his arms at the birds. Vultures flew off Bruce, whom Jack recognized only by the Creedence Clearwater Revival patch on his shoulder. He had no face. Jack stumbled. Next to Bruce's body lay a piece of the instrument panel. But where was Dad? The rest of the fuselage lay like a beached dolphin, its aluminum shell charred and broken.

Then Jack saw him.

Dad was in the plane. Though the cockpit was all but destroyed, Dad's body hadn't been hurled out. He was jammed against an unbroken part of the cockpit window, his face burned but his body protected from the birds, for now.

Up to that instant Jack had believed his dad was alive. Now there was no doubt. His father was dead. More vultures began to land on the fuselage, tilting the plane's nose downward, scraping it against the cliff. Jack screamed and lunged at the birds with a branch, beating them off. But the plane tilted more when the birds flew away, and Dad's body fell forward, his dead eyes open and looking directly at Jack.

The birds reassembled. Jack beat them off again, then sank to the ground and wept. He held his face against the dusty rock, muddying it with his tears, not wanting to die. He felt horribly guilty.

Had he not fallen from the plane, he might have been able to help Dad and Bruce.

Finally, he sat up and noticed that Stone Boy was staring at him from a nearby rock top, his hair bristling and his eyes wide.

The birds had landed on the fuselage again, rocking the plane and making it slide farther down. The cracks in the fuselage creaked as they opened wider. Bits of paper spilled out of the plane, and Jack leaped to his feet and jumped for them, still hoping absurdly for some message from his father. More of the flight map, and some notes in Dad's hand, jotted on sheets from a legal pad. And a color photo of a smiling African woman with a note written on it: *Bruce, happy birthday!* The wind tore the photo away. Jack crumpled Dad's notes into his tattered pocket. The birds kept crowding onto the plane, causing the fuselage to creak under their weight. Jack tried to think rationally: Rescuers would be looking for a wreck. If the plane's body remained intact and didn't slip off the cliff, they would easily be able to spot it from the air.

Jack decided to stay near the wreck, but the idea of being so close to his father's body was almost too painful to bear. He spread out what was left of the map and examined it, the Witch's Pot looming on the right side of the page. He saw the Ruaha Natural Park almost at the opposite end of the map and remembered that they had flown for three hours due west, which was roughly three hundred miles. Between the park and the Witch's Pot, Jack didn't see a single road or town marked on the map.

Stone Boy grunted from the top of the rock. Jack looked up at him. All at once Jack realized how much the events that had brought the two of them together had disrupted Stone Boy's life irreparably. The thought was so sudden and clear, so scientific, that it made Jack ache for his father even more.

"Go away," Jack said hoarsely. "Go away—you can't help here."

At first Stone Boy didn't move. Then he darted behind the rock and reappeared in seconds. He'd caught another little rodent. He sat staring at the wreckage as he bit into his meal. The plane shifted down several more feet. Jack wanted to pull the bodies of Bruce and Dad out of the plane and bury them. He ran to the Bergen, retrieved the aardvark, then dashed back to the plane and crawled under the fuselage, looking for the best way to get inside. Jack searched desperately until he found an opening, and embedded the aardvark in the fuselage in an attempt to wedge the opening wider. He realized that he probably couldn't bury the bodies in the rock cliff face even if he was able to get them out of the cockpit. He listened to the hungry birds' ruckus, wondering how he could stop the wreck from breaking into any more pieces than it already had. If he could find a couple of smaller rocks, maybe he could jam them under the nose and keep it from sliding off the cliff face.

Jack began to feel incredibly exhausted at the thought of this task. He searched the rocks for Stone Boy but did not see him. *He's gone back to his own life in the wild*, Jack thought. He felt tears on his face and cried bitterly, knowing that no one could hear him except for the birds and beasts so preoccupied with their next meal. "Dad, what were you thinking, bringing us here?" he sobbed. "How am I going to get home?" Jack rolled out from under the plane. "I can't do this without you, Dad. I can't."

THE SUN SLIPPED down, tinting the world red.

The bigger birds had flown away, but smaller, brightly colored ones perched on the plane, slipping in and out of small holes around the cockpit.

Jack paced around the plane to see if he could detach anything useful. But it was all burned. He slid partway into the cockpit through the broken glass. Everywhere there were sharp pieces of metal he could peel off with his hand. He gathered several of them.

He gripped something on Dad's belt and pulled it free. It was a knife, twice as large as Bruce's gift. A big bush knife, its blade discolored from the fire. The patterned plastic of the handle had melted, but it had cooled and resolidified. It was misshapen and ugly, but usable nonetheless.

Dad's compass was still strapped to his wrist. Jack tried to unfasten it, but the clasp was melted and fused. Dad's voice echoed clearly in his mind: *one shot.* Jack reached into his father's pocket and withdrew crumpled, singed notes. His own name sprang out at him: *Jack—*

Wiping his eyes with dirty hands, he read: *I'm still hoping for one big discovery. The Witch's Pot is*

72

like nothing scientists have seen before. Who knows what treasures have survived during millions of years in isolation? Officially, of course, I'm here to tag lions. But I wouldn't be surprised if Jack saw through the ruse. Not a really convincing cover.

Jack froze. His dad wasn't here to tag lions? Then what *was* he looking for?

Jack folded the note and put it in the Bergen. He put his dad's knife in the Bergen too. Struggling to fit his body through the narrow hole in the fuselage, he lowered himself out of the plane and staggered away from it. He set the Bergen down in a dip in the bare rock and laid his head on it. He didn't want to think about how Dad had brought him out here and put him in harm's way, but still hadn't confided in him.

—‖—

N<small>IGHT FELL</small> and the moon sailed up into the sky. Jack heard creatures in the dark, claws on the rock. He wondered if it was the baboon troop. He pulled himself out of the dip in the rock he'd curled into and looked over the edge of the cliff. Two lionesses were climbing toward the crash site.

Without even thinking, Jack ran to the instrument

panel, lifted it, and hurled it at the big cats. It crashed against the rock, startling the lions, who leaped back to the ground.

Satisfied that he had discouraged them, Jack huddled on the rock, amazed how cold the night on the savanna was. He tried to fall asleep for a few minutes, until he heard something scraping across the rocks. He jumped to his feet again. The bright moon illuminated the plane—moving! It slid down the incline, the fuselage cracking apart. Jack ran toward it, but the plane swept past him and hurtled off the cliff.

Below, a thick acacia grove shook violently as the plane crashed into it, but then the foliage gathered again, like water swallowing a sinking vessel. The leaves shivered, then were still. The plane had disappeared from view entirely.

Jack lay down, powerless, in the lingering stench of the burned plane. Below, the night was loud with roaring lions. Was it going to be like this every night from now on? How many nights? He had to make a plan. Now that the only landmark large enough to signal a plane was gone, he didn't know where he should wait to be rescued. At least from the ledge he might be visible to a plane. On the other hand, lions were everywhere. He heard other animals too. Hyenas chuckled, and a jackal or wild dog howled nearby. How did Stone Boy do it? Why wasn't the little ape afraid? Or was he?

Jack was horribly thirsty again, and hungrier than he had ever been before. He knew he had to go down into the grassland and find something to eat, anything, before his body shut down. At dawn tomorrow, first thing, he would start the hunt.

PART 3

WITCH'S POT, WESTERN TANZANIA

CHAPTER ONE

In the morning Jack began his descent from the cliff. Near the bottom he saw a tree being savaged by a troop of baboons, fighting and screeching and plucking nuts from the branches. Mungongo nuts! Dad had mentioned they were edible.

Jack ran up to the tree, slipped the Bergen off his shoulder, and swung it like a nunchaku. The baboons dove at him, scratching his chest and legs. They bared their teeth in his face, growling viciously. He pulled Dad's knife out and hacked the air with the naked blade: The closest baboon ran into it with his shoulder. Blood spurted from the wound as the injured ape fell back. The horde screeched and withdrew. Jack pulled nuts from the tree, trying to avoid the tooth-marked ones. He tried to pry the shells open, but they slipped from his fingers into the dirt. Picking up a nut, he rubbed it on the front of his pants and tried to bite it open, but it was as solid as a bullet. He spotted a nut that was already opened, so he picked it up and popped the kernel into his mouth. It slipped down his throat before he could taste it. Then Jack spotted a whole pile of opened mungongo nuts, abandoned by the baboons. He ate another kernel, this time chewing it. The flesh was surprisingly sweet. Jack sat down in the dirt, eating kernel after kernel. He wiggled his tongue into the shells' niches, appreciating nature's genius in packing nutrients into the tightest possible space.

He stuffed a whole handful of kernels into his mouth, chewing hard until his jaw muscles ached. Using the knife's blade, he dug into the cracks carefully, since he couldn't afford to blunt the knife. There were mungongo trees all around him.

He could easily pick enough mungongo nuts to fill his Bergen and then some. Would that be enough food to trek out of there? Jack wondered.

The smallest nuts, which he couldn't open with the knife, he carried to a rock that was low and flat, like a tabletop. He held them against the rock with two fingers and hit them with a stone. If he hit them on the apex of the shell, they cracked nicely into two halves. Jack grinned as he worked.

At his feet there was a muddy puddle filled with empty mungongo shells.

He cupped water in his hands and drank. It was bitter and tasted like minerals. *Better get used to it,* Jack thought. He took the plastic bottle out of the Bergen and filled it with muddy water. The bottle, made to be disposable, was now one of his prized possessions. Specks of brown swirled, settling slowly. If he held the bottle still, the water and dirt began to separate, but what was the use? Jack took another swig and hoped the water wasn't full of parasites or bacteria. Getting sick was not an option. Besides, Stone Boy drank dirty water and ate raw meat, and he seemed just fine.

Jack wondered why Stone Boy was alone. He

had to have parents, obviously, and probably siblings, too. His own ape clan must be out there somewhere. How far away could they be?

Jack tried to focus. If rescuers did not come for him in the next few days, he would have to make a very important decision—to continue waiting or try to hike out. If he chose to wait, he'd have to learn how to protect himself. If he chose to make the journey out of the Witch's Pot, he'd probably have to hunt for food on the way. In the meantime, Jack's mission was to keep eating and drinking. Whatever he chose to do, he had to regain his strength and maintain his stamina. Once he was in good shape, if he hadn't been spotted already, he could try to climb the rim and head east until he found a road.

Then he remembered: He had to climb not one, but two storm-lashed rims.

He'd have to be strong enough to stand up to the winds, or they could hurl him off the heights.

Jack's thumb hurt. He'd nicked it cracking nuts. The cut was tiny, but if it got infected . . . He pictured his finger swelling up, the infection spreading.

He was panicking. He tried to take deep, calming breaths. Just then, the grass ahead of him shook. A lion slunk out and limped to the puddle, where he put his mouth down and drank, then leaped up on the rock where Jack had cracked the nuts. Seemingly ready for a nap, he lay down on his belly. With scars and mangy patches everywhere, the lion looked old, and when he yawned, his steak-knife teeth looked very yellow. As the lion reclined, another male sauntered up—smaller and mangier. He climbed the rock and lay down next to his companion. Jack crept back behind the mungongo tree and slid to the ground, not daring to breathe. He had a large knife, but what good would it really do him if the lions smelled him? What would he do if that hungry, yellow flame kindled in their eyes and they sprang on him?

He waited and tried to come up with a plan in case the lions attacked. Jack tried to imagine what Stone Boy would do. Stone Boy lived and hunted in a place swarming with lions, and yet he'd managed to drag Jack, feverish and bleeding, out of harm's way. Stone Boy, Jack realized, didn't just react. He strategized. The lions were ready for an afternoon nap, apparently oblivious to Jack's presence. Baffled, Jack suddenly realized that they couldn't smell him. The baboons had disguised his odor! *I lucked out,* he thought.

Stone Boy might have lucked out this way, hiding from lions behind the stench of some other animal. Perhaps luck was how he had learned survival strategies. *I'm learning too,* Jack thought. A few moments later, the larger lion opened his eyes and roared softly. Perhaps calling for lionesses. The lion had bags under his eyes like an old man. He would roar once, then prick up his ears for a response. The other lion roared too, tentatively, like an apprentice learning from his master. Both waited for a response from the bush, but there was no reply. They got up, sniffed the air, and roared again. Still nothing. The lions finally resettled on the rock and put their heads on their forepaws, while Jack crawled away on his stomach. When he reached what he thought was a safe distance, he got up and took off at a full run.

He finally galloped by a large tree. He broke off a branch and continued walking, whittling it with Dad's knife as he went. Then he took a piece of fuselage, jagged and burned to blue, out of his Bergen. He fitted it on the end of the branch, curling the bottom of the metal around to fasten it. Now Jack had a spear. He'd climb a hill the next morning and try to get his bearings. *Maybe*, he thought, *a rescue plane could see me more easily on a hilltop*. Until then, he knew, he had to keep moving. Ahead, the bushes grew in tall clumps, and thousands of birds were alighting on them, bending the branches and making a tremendous noise. They were small, perhaps a variety of partridge or quail. If he had to lie down and rest, Jack thought, he should do it close to the birds. That way if anything snuck up on him, they'd start such a racket, Jack would know instantly that a predator was approaching.

Where was Stone Boy? Jack wondered. Had the sight of the crashed plane frightened him off permanently? Jack marched with his sack strapped to his left shoulder and his right fist clutching the whittled branch, aiming the spear tip ahead. Stone Boy's makeshift sutures had worked, and although Jack's arm was still sore, it was healing, and he no longer felt feverish.

As he walked, Jack's eyes started to close. They were even more tired than his legs. Could he lie down and rest a little? Where were those birds? He told his arm to aim the spear ahead, told his legs to keep walking, and closed his eyes. *Discipline*, Jack thought. *I won't fall asleep.*

Nearby, he heard a kind of chuckle.

He opened his eyes.

Stone Boy stood two yards away, next to a bank of tall grass. Jack laughed, reached inside the Bergen, and held out a mungongo nut for Stone Boy. Stone Boy looked at him, curious yet unsurprised. *Has he been stalking me?* Jack wondered. The little ape swiped the nut so fast, his dirty fingernails scratched Jack's hand. He folded his lips back, stuck the nut under a tooth, and chewed. Then he reached for Jack's crude spear and twittered excitedly, not sure what to make of it.

"It's the best I could do," Jack said matter-of-factly, trying to stand tall and look determined.

Stone Boy didn't look convinced.

"Look," Jack said. "I just ran into a couple of lions and got away fine all by myself, thank you. I can make it here, with or without you."

He strutted past Stone Boy, who suddenly jumped in front of him and grabbed his arms, gripping them tightly. The curiosity in his eyes was bottomless, yet he was staring at something in the distance. Jack followed Stone Boy's gaze to the tall grass, where a lioness sat on her haunches, sniffing the air. Behind her there were half a dozen more lionesses, with several tottering cubs. Their faces were all turned in the same direction, listening closely. Jack heard the males roar some ways off. *Rowowow-oo, rowowow-oo!*

The lionesses listened. They blended into the grass so well, Jack realized, that he would have walked straight into the pride if not for Stone Boy. One lioness, small and girlish-looking, ventured a little roar of response: *wow-wooow*. But the larger mothers with cubs turned and hissed fiercely, and the youngster was instantly quiet. Jack stepped back, then crouched down. The way Stone Boy's arms hung by his body, away from his sides—were there hunting stones in his armpits? Jack looked around for a tree. Lions were too heavy to climb trees, but the only ones around, the mungongo trees, were far behind him now.

To the left of the tall grass he saw big heaps of black flesh, and tails and ears slapping bugs off. Water buffaloes, a whole big herd, rolling closer. Hearing their bellows, an older lioness emerged from the tall grass. Looking crabby and cynical, she sniffed the air, saw the two bipeds, and began to creep toward them. Jack raised his spear, ready to use it against the advancing lioness, but the aluminum tip fell off. Stone Boy narrowed his eyes at his strange companion, the intruder who had warded off a lion by yelling at it. He waited, as if to see if Jack had a plan, and when nothing happened, Stone Boy raised a hunting stone and shifted it in his fingers to find a solid grip.

Then he turned toward Jack, sizing him up again, and lowered the stone. This was Jack's turn, he seemed to say. Jack's chance to prove himself. Whether Stone Boy's expectation was connected to having seen the crash site, glimpsing the world that Jack belonged to—gruesome and yet breathtakingly novel—Jack could only guess. In a flash, he remembered that Stone Boy had watched him tumble out of the plane. He had fallen, quite literally, from the sky. Jack wondered if Stone Boy thought he was capable of magic. *Show your stuff,* the ape's eyes seemed to urge.

Stone Boy tucked the stone back in his armpit.

Trembling, Jack still tried to appraise the lioness's intent: She didn't seem hungry, but she crept closer and closer to them. Sweat broke out on Jack's forehead. He smelled his own fear, warm and rank. The feline smelled it too. Jack yelled hoarsely, waving his arms, but the lioness didn't stop.

Grabbing Stone Boy's arm, Jack turned and took off toward the water buffaloes. One appeared before him, eyes half open, nostrils flaring. But Jack wasn't worried about the buffaloes. They were cows! Their musky smell hit him all at once. He slipped between two massive beasts, bumped against one, hit it with his fists, and glanced back. Stone Boy, too, had scrambled between the buffaloes, his eyes like little coals, dying to see what Jack would do. Jack tore the Bergen off his shoulder and swatted the cows with it. Good choice. The buffaloes bellowed; the calves hurtled ahead, with their mothers close behind them. The herd charged toward the lions, bellowing more urgently.

The males, horns forward, shot ahead to protect their young.

A hoof came down on Jack's left boot, full on. He fell, and the buffaloes parted around him, moving on.

Stone Boy scurried in and tugged Jack out of the crowd. Jack gasped in pain and looked down. He'd lost his left boot, and there was a stabbing pain in his left ankle. Probably sprained. Once they made it out of the fray, Jack sat down and pulled his other boot off. Stone Boy squatted beside him and screeched: *Eee eee eee eee eee!*

Jack's plan had worked. He had chased the big cows into the pride, and now, peering between buffalo legs, Jack and Stone Boy saw the fleeing lions, cubs in their mothers' jaws. All that was amazing enough to Stone Boy, but more impressive still were Jack's feet, no longer hidden in his boots. He screamed excitedly.

Suddenly, the earth beneath them shook. The buffaloes were coming straight toward them.

Stone Boy clutched Jack's elbow and pulled him up, but they lost their balance and fell. Jack put his weight on his bad foot and yelled. Stone Boy snatched him around the waist and tried to lift him onto his back.

"Put me down," Jack gasped. "Take care of yourself!" Stone Boy growled and dove to the ground. Then he began pulling up grass.

"What are you doing?" Jack yelled. "Stop it! We have to get out of here!" Jack tried to move out of the buffaloes' path, but his first step sent a spark of pain up his spine.

Stone Boy worked furiously, grabbing handfuls of roots and grass and tossing them behind him. Over his shoulder he glared at Jack as if urging him: *You do it too! Get going!* Jack dove onto his stomach and followed Stone Boy's lead. Again and again, Stone Boy dashed to collect rocks and pebbles nearby and tossed them on the pile. As the buffaloes charged toward them, Jack, gritting his teeth, threw whatever was within arm's reach onto the makeshift rampart. Just before the first bulls slammed into them, Stone Boy yanked Jack to the top of the pile, and they braced themselves against each other. Jack squeezed his eyes shut, ready to be trampled. But at the last second the panicked column of buffaloes cleaved in two, flowing around the "island." Moving like galleons, some veered to the right, others to the left.

Astonished and shaking, Jack watched the herd pass. Moving swiftly around the obstacle, the buffaloes' sides bumped occasionally, but they avoided full-on collisions. A calf strayed onto the island. Stone Boy slapped its rump, and instantly several cows bellowed and the calf hustled back to the herd.

As the herd slowed, the bipeds finally sat down, chests still heaving. Jack was so ecstatic that they had survived without being flattened, he laughed, picked up a handful of grass, and threw it over his head. Stone Boy performed his own celebration, hooting and stomping his feet rapidly.

"He's so smart!" Jack muttered under his breath. But before he could give it another thought, that lioness appeared between two columns of buffaloes. Low to the ground, she crouched between countless hooves, moving one pace at a time, so the buffaloes wouldn't crush her. Her ears were pulled back on her skull and her eyes narrowed tightly.

Jack gauged the pain in his ankle and realized

he couldn't make a run for it. "Beat it!" he yelled at the feline. The lion started to retreat backwards when a buffalo trampled her hind legs. She yowled in pain and turned and crept away, vanishing into the throng of buffaloes.

"Ha ha! It worked!" Jack felt fearless. In triumph, he threw his arm around Stone Boy, who clucked in surprise but didn't push Jack aside. He and Stone Boy stood next to each other and looked out over the savanna, ready to face the wild together.

CHAPTER TWO

That afternoon the herd scattered around Stone Boy's little island, grazing for hours, then settling down to chew their cud and rest. Jack knew they wouldn't leave before they depleted all the grass in the area, which might be tomorrow or the day after. Jack felt relieved at the thought that he and Stone Boy might be protected from the lions for one more day. Still, his ankle, which had swollen up like a balloon, hurt terribly.

Later, a perfect boat-shaped half-moon floated into the sky. Jack tried to fall asleep beside Stone

Boy, close enough to feel the warmth from his body, but the stars were so bright and clear, he couldn't keep his eyes closed. Jack finally sat up. As he looked out over the herd, the silhouette of the lioness rose out of the grass. Jack figured that she had concealed herself all that time, silent and still, so as not to provoke another stampede. Now that the herd was resting and inattentive, she could sneak up on Jack and Stone Boy.

Her glittering eyes reflecting the moonlight, the lioness gazed at Jack, who stared back at her. *I should jump up and yell,* he thought. *I could wake the buffaloes and have her squashed like a rag.* But the pain in his ankle made him remember how lucky he had been today. His father's words came back to him: *one shot.* Maybe he should grant the defeated lioness this one chance to survive. Still staring her down, Jack moved to stand up. The lioness darted away, trotted off into the night, and vanished.

Jack settled back down next to Stone Boy, who turned in his sleep, spread out his arms, and sighed. Jack felt at ease too. He had a friend in the savanna.

PART 4

OUTER RIM OF THE WITCH'S POT, WESTERN TANZANIA

CHAPTER ONE

Two planes struggled to gain altitude against the outer rim of the Witch's Pot. The clouds, indicating brewing storms, formed an almost uninterrupted barrier. Flying the lead plane, a Helio Courier as old as Alan Conran's, was Frank Aoyama. He tried to catch the updrafts, hoping to break across the peaks into the quieter sky between the two rims. This task would be extremely difficult for him, but it would be nearly impossible for the unseasoned pilot of the second plane, a twin-engine Twin Otter. The pilot, a former military flier, had no experience with the temperamental winds blowing off the rims of the Witch's Pot. He did his best to follow Professor Aoyama's flight path as closely as he could, but the bobbing and weaving required to keep up caused the Otter's paramedics to heave into their airsickness bags.

The only person who was not sick was Nancy Gwara, the head of the paramedics' team. A native of Queens, New York, Nancy had moved to Tanzania and married a local businessman. "There's no better training for a bumpy ride than driving an ambulance around Queens," Nancy joked.

"See anything, Professor Aoyama?" she said into the radio.

"Nothing," Frank replied tonelessly.

Alan Conran had been out of radio contact for six days.

The day before, the two planes had flown for hours outside the Pot, pushing deep west, then turning north. Finally they came full circle, having spotted nothing on the ground.

For the Otter's pilot, the disappearance was a closed case. "Professor Conran crashed. This or that side of the rim—does it really matter?" he argued before the planes had even started out on the second day of the search. "The foliage in that place can hide a wreck completely. Even if the fuselage caught fire, it rains so much up there, whatever was burning would be extinguished pretty fast."

Sensing her dedication from the start, Frank had looked at Nancy Gwara for help.

"The government lent us to you for two days," she said. "Let's make the most of our time, Professor."

Nancy knew that they were looking for two adults and one thirteen-year-old, the professor's son. The pilot had studied the lay of the land, as had Professor Conran, but could a boy survive in the bush on his own?

"My own husband was raised tribally," she told Frank. "He went on the walk, and he made it—three days alone in the bush at age nine."

Nancy was not as pessimistic as the pilot. The bush hid its casualties with a vengeance, she knew, but she was passionate about going out on rescues—this one especially. She had attended one of Alan's lectures about Tanzania's pristine habitats, and the man had piqued her imagination with his ideas. In isolated environments that had changed little since the Pleistocene epoch, Conran had theorized, plants and animals that scientists had long considered extinct might still exist. He was clearly a driven man, Nancy remembered.

After several hours of flying along the slopes of the outer rim, the search team had found nothing. Nancy sighed, her hope fading. The radio crackled.

"We have to try to cross over the rim," Frank yelled over the noise of his engine. "It's the only place Alan could be."

"That's beyond the call of duty," the Otter's pilot shouted. "This job doesn't pay me enough to do something that stupid."

"Look," Frank answered. "We've canvassed every inch of these slopes and the plane's not here. I'm willing to bet that my Helio can make it across, and if that's the case, your shiny new Otter should have no trouble." Frank knew they needed to extend the search, or else they'd have to declare Alan's party as "missing, presumed dead," without any evidence that their plane had gone down.

"Fine," the pilot begrudgingly conceded. "But if

anything happens to my plane or my passengers, I'm holding you to blame."

The pilot knew that failing to recover the downed plane would reflect poorly on him. The Tanzanian government had offered his skills as its best contribution to rescuing Alan and Bruce. The Tanzanian government supported Frank's community of scientists because they brought the region renown and income. The pilot had agreed to the mission because it seemed like a good career move. He'd given little thought to the weather factor. There was nothing he could do now but follow the Helio into the Witch's Pot.

"Why's he twisting like that?" the pilot complained, straining to stay behind Frank, whose plane snaked from right to left and back again.

"Could be following a river, a mountain range—some geological feature that Professor Conran was studying," Nancy yelled as water and wind pelted the Otter's nose.

"I don't think so," the pilot shot back. "With this rain, there's very little visibility."

Frank's plane bucked in the wind, and the Otter's pilot struggled to keep his wings level. The cockpit shook, and Nancy gripped the armrests of her seat with both hands. But then, with the Otter close on its tail, the Helio broke through the storm clouds and Frank rocked the plane's wings up and down, like a puppy shaking water off its coat. He gunned forward over the lush green of the savanna.

The pilot was right. Frank hadn't been following a geological feature. Before his last communication with the Otter's pilot, he'd realized that the secret to finding Alan might be right on his dashboard. Frank's Helio had been used for animal tagging too—its instrument panel contained a radar identical to Alan's. A blip on the screen would tell him exactly where the lions Alan had tagged were.

The radar's computer contained a log, and each blip appeared with the date and time of the tagging. Before he'd gone over the rim, Frank had spotted three tagged animals on the outer slopes. The dates showed they had been tagged during earlier flights. Frank had an idea—what if Alan had flown *inside* the crater to tag? If he'd been successful, a blip would surely show up on Frank's screen.

Safely beyond the Witch's Pot's outer rim, Frank was staring hopefully at the radar when a red light lit up next to the fuel meter. Time to land and refuel. Frank chose a stretch of smooth grassland and landed the plane.

When the Otter landed beside him, the pilot barreled out of his cockpit.

As Frank pulled a canister of gasoline from the Helio's hold and siphoned it into the fuel tank, the Otter's pilot charged toward him. He was followed at a run by Nancy Gwara, panicked that the pilot's quick temper could result in spilled blood miles from the nearest hospital. But as the Otter's pilot towered over Frank, the scientist smiled like a sage and said: "Thanks for putting up with all that shaking. Now I'm going to go up again and take a look while you guys catch your breath. Radio if you have any brilliant ideas." He motioned at the sky, strangely calm between the rims.

"You have one hour," the Otter's pilot barked.

Frank waved and jumped back into the cockpit.

CHAPTER TWO

B ack in the sky, Frank wondered what exactly Alan's lion project was about. He remembered Alan's theory, that lions were deeply affected by the rapidly changing environment and by the encroachment of humans into their habitat. Alan had suggested that a wild lion cub was less likely to survive to maturity than a human living in a war zone.

Not much for them to worry about here, Frank thought, spotting clusters of tan shapes on rocks and near water holes.

He looked at the console, watching the radar

sweep across the screen. Then a flickering dot appeared. A tagged lion was somewhere on the ground nearby.

"I knew it," Frank exclaimed. Alan had crossed the outer rim! If the conditions at the peak had been anything like what Frank had just encountered, Alan's pilot must have made some risky maneuvers to navigate through them successfully. Foolhardy maybe, but Alan's choice had extended his research area by a couple of thousand square miles. Frank had reread the research permit request that morning, along with a whole deskful of Alan's papers, in search of clues. In his permit request, Alan had asked to tag prides on the outer rim only. But here it was right on Frank's screen—proof that Alan had taken his quest farther.

Frank flew north, excited that he was on the right track. At the same time, he was terrified that at any moment, pieces of a downed Helio might appear on the dusty landscape below. Frank waited for another blip to appear on the radar, but the screen was dark. Had Alan tagged only one lion before succumbing to whatever mysterious fate had kept him out of radio contact for the last six days?

Though he didn't see any wreckage from the air, Frank knew that a small plane like Alan's could fragment so badly on impact, and the pieces would be so scattered, that there wouldn't have to be a clearly identifiable crash site. Foliage, as the pilot had reminded him, would naturally camouflage the plane. But Alan knew that. If anything happened to him in the bush, he would no doubt try to land where he would be seen by rescuers. Maybe, Frank imagined, Alan had had a radio problem and an engine malfunction at the same time and been forced to land in a forested area. That would explain why he hadn't sent an SOS call and why the plane was nowhere to be seen. Maybe Alan and Bruce were somewhere below him, trying to repair the engine so they could take off again. There was water down there—Frank could tell by how green the flora was. There would be food, too, plenty to sustain all of them.

Still, Frank wondered: Why would Alan risk his life—and stranger still, his son's—to tag lions inside the crater?

"What were you really after, my friend?" Frank muttered softly.

He doubted that Alan, though he was known to have taken some risks in his career, would have intentionally put his son in harm's way. Although he sometimes felt guilty about not seeing Jack more often, Alan loved his son more than anything. Everyone at the center knew that.

Frank looped back around and flew south. He saw lion prides below, but his radar screen remained blank. As Frank surveyed the terrain, he was overcome by the majesty of this place. It looked so ancient, yet so lush and alive. The peaks of the inner rim were shrouded in mist, as beautiful as they were dangerous. Could Alan have taken his expedition even farther? With Jack on board, what could possibly have driven him to cross that perilous boundary?

I have to come back in a larger plane, he thought.

Alan, Frank realized, had kept secrets from him. There was only one thing Alan cared about enough to put himself and his son in harm's way: the possibility of a major fossil site. *Australopithecus afarensis*, one of the most ancient hominid species ever discovered in Africa, was Alan's research specialty. Had he found some sign of it here? Or had the mystery of that great unknown led the scientist across the second rim? Was his lion-tagging project just a front? *I've got to find out what happened,* Frank thought.

He realized that, for today, his decision had been made for him. The second rim, obscured by steely black clouds, was impassable.

Frank flew back and brought the plane down beside the parked Twin Otter. The paramedics were staring up at the fuselage of the Helio as if to decipher in its shine the result of the search.

"Nothing, Professor?" Nancy Gwara asked, a useless question, since the answer was written all over Frank's face as he stepped out of his cockpit.

Frank shook his head.

"So we go back to the center," the Otter's pilot urged.

Frank nodded. He did not have the energy for an argument.

"If you want my help tomorrow, you've got it," Nancy said.

"Thanks, Nancy. All right," he said, turning to the pilot and the other paramedics, "looks like the search is over for today."

PART 5

WITCH'S POT, WESTERN TANZANIA

CHAPTER ONE

That night it rained—on the savanna and the herds, and on Jack and Stone Boy, who slept back-to-back. When Jack awoke, the water buffalo herd had moved on and moles and rodents were burrowing up from the soaked earth. Stone Boy woke and chased one, killed it with his teeth, and brought back half for Jack.

I need protein, Jack thought. *Even uncooked protein. I might as well try my luck with this mole.* He bit into the warm raw meat and felt sick immediately.

Stone Boy ran off, then came thumping back,

carrying an egg that he cracked smack onto Jack's lips. Jack ate the egg, raw and full of nutrients, and felt better. Still hobbled by his swollen ankle, he limped a few paces across the grass and saw a buffalo cow giving birth. He crawled to a watering hole, where more moms and newborns waded. The moms nuzzled the babies and licked their fur. Jack looked around: no lions. As the sky cleared, the water hole looked blue and inviting. Jack imagined he was somewhere else, somewhere safe.

I'm by the swimming pool in Meg's backyard in Pasadena, he thought. *Meg's dad is making hamburgers on the grill.* As Jack was conjuring the delicious smell of sizzling meat, Stone Boy snuck up and elbowed him into the water. Jack surfaced immediately. Stone Boy bared his teeth in laughter. Jack grabbed Stone Boy's feet and pulled him into the water. Stone Boy swam poorly, dog-paddling ineffectively. He tried to catch up with Jack, who breaststroked away in long smooth pulls. Opening his eyes underwater, Jack saw hippos: two submerged, three surfacing with leaves on their heads. When the boys kicked to the surface, a newborn hippo floated by, shiny like gunmetal. Stone Boy scampered ashore, but when Jack tried to wade out too, Stone Boy gave him a hard kick. Jack fell back into the water. He got out and punched Stone Boy in the shoulder. They sized each other up, but Stone Boy didn't punch back; he just sat there, wispy hair moving in the breeze.

"You want to know how strong I am, huh?" Jack said.

Stone Boy watched his mouth, captivated by the sound of Jack's voice.

"I talk. It's one of the best things I do. Do you like it?"

Stone Boy emitted an *eeee* of four different pitches, from low to high.

Jack laughed. "We're quite a team, aren't we?"

Jack walked around the watering hole, determined to ignore the pain in his ankle. "Nothing's going to stop me," he said. "I'm going to make another spear—one that won't fall apart this time! Then I'm going to walk back to that plane and find a cigarette lighter, or matches, or a few bits of glass—that's all I need. I'll make a fire. When the rescue plane comes, they'll see it." Stone Boy kept his eyes on Jack, appearing to process the words.

Jack studied his face. "What are you doing here, anyway? How come you're alone?" Stone Boy sat mute but attentive. "Right. Good answer."

Jack knelt down, scooped up some water, and washed his hands and face. Stone Boy imitated his movements, splashing water on his face too. When some water went up his nose, Stone Boy coughed and spat furiously. Jack laughed and walked over to the tree where his Bergen and boots were. He examined the boots, battered but still usable. Jack put them on, tugging one gingerly over his sprained ankle. He would have to go barefoot when they fell apart. Then, trampled in the grass, the dictionary's glossy cover glinted at him. Jack flipped through the pages and then tucked the book carefully into his backpack. The pen and the notepad were thankfully still attached.

Sawing the knife into green wood, Jack cut two lean branches off a young tree. He sharpened the knife on a rock, chose the straightest branch, and spent the rest of the morning carefully whittling it into a spear.

After watching awhile, Stone Boy picked up a rock, took the other branch, and cut his thumb raw trying to do what Jack was doing.

"You're competitive. And quick to learn new skills. That's good, but how many thousands of years more would it have taken you to make a spear on your own?"

Dad had told Jack about scientists intruding on their subjects. Researchers wanted to study Amazonian tribes like the Mayorunas—isolated groups that had never encountered outsiders. After the researchers arrived, the "contacted Indians" gradually, but permanently, changed their ways. They abandoned their traditional dress and put on T-shirts and pants. They moved from villages to towns, and made their living selling "tribal Indian food" to tourists. They would never go back to their old ways.

"I don't want to change you, Stone Boy," Jack said. "But two heads are better than one, and I have to find a way out of here. I'm guessing you're on your way somewhere too. You have to have some family here. You didn't just fall out of the sky—*I* did. Sorry, bad joke." Stone Boy blinked, as if in agreement. "C'mon, let's go."

He walked, still limping a little, ahead of Stone

Boy, back toward the rock ledge. The plane had slid from the ledge and crashed into the acacia grove below, and now Jack tried to forget that his father had ever been in it. *I need to make a fire*, Jack thought. *And I need what's in the plane.*

=‖=

THERE WAS A clearing in the middle of the acacia grove, where sunlight streamed down, onto the broken fuselage.

White-whiskered forest pigs dug their snouts into the wreckage as if looking for roots.

Something crunched under Jack's boot. Broken glass.

He picked up the shards and shoved them into his Bergen. He saw a chunk of mirror and picked that up too. Just what he needed. He could leave the wreckage to the scavengers.

But just as he turned to go, a lioness emerged from the trees, lunged, and caught one of the pigs. The other pigs squealed and tried to run away, but suddenly there were lionesses all around them, pushing their cubs forward, bumping them with their noses toward the pigs, trying to teach them how to hunt.

Jack took out the piece of mirror, caught a sun ray in it, and aimed it at a cub's eyes. Blinded, the cub yowled. Jack moved that beacon across the cats' faces, and they stopped what they were doing immediately. One lioness started toward Jack, pricked her paw on a piece of aluminum, and groaned in pain. The other lionesses, unsure of what danger they faced, called their cubs. The pride abandoned its hunting session.

Some revenge, Jack thought.

Standing behind Jack, Stone Boy held up a hunting stone. Jack's performance with the mirror had surprised him so much, he'd cried out in amazement and run off. Jack threw the mirror shard back into the Bergen and caught up with his partner.

He found him on the edge of a ravine, clutching the spear that he hadn't yet whittled completely and staring toward Jack in frightened wonderment. "The glass, it's for fire, Stone Boy. You know fire, don't you? The savanna catches fire from heat."

Stone Boy stared back.

"Come on. You can help me, Stone Boy."

Stone Boy stood, still uncertain, and smelled

the air. He pointed toward the ravine that twisted below them.

They crept to the edge and peered over.

More lions, below. One lioness, and two males.

The lioness had been cornered by the males. Growling, tail switching, she let them smell her. Jack recognized her from her limp: the lioness who was injured during the buffalo stampede. He recognized the two males, too—he'd seen them near the mungongo tree the day he left the wreck. Amazing, he thought—the bush was filling with familiar faces—predators' faces, but familiar nonetheless.

Quick and mean, the younger lion pounced on the lioness's neck. She snapped at him, but he dragged her into the dirt, snarling. *Don't go down! Don't go down!* Jack found himself rooting for the lioness. The older male snapped at her chin, but she ripped her bleeding face out of her attacker's fangs and uttered a long broken whine.

From up ahead, another lion grunted. It sounded like a female. The cornered lioness cried out as if regaining hope. The males batted their tails and corralled her up the ravine. Unfurling her tongue, she licked at her torn chin.

More unseen lionesses called from the direction of the acacia grove. Maybe the pride with cubs, the pride that had scavenged the plane, recognized the voice.

The older male lion nudged the captured lioness's side, pushing her toward the unsuspecting pride.

Stone Boy turned to Jack. His eyes were urgent and he pointed back toward the grassland where buffaloes grazed: *Let's go back—we're safer there.*

But Jack shook his head. "We can't go back. Anywhere we go, we'll run into lions. We have to go forward, not back!"

They heard an ugly chuckle. They saw hyenas, trailing just a few yards behind them.

Jack hesitated, weighing his options. As much as they feared the lions, they could use them as well. Jack ran along the trail of paw prints that the lions had left behind them. He waved at Stone Boy to follow, and they both ran until they saw the three lions again. As soon as the hyenas smelled the lions, they retreated.

The lioness was still leading, while the males escorted her.

They want to take over the pride! Jack guessed.

As they ran after the lions, Jack felt like Dad was right beside him. *You're right, Jack. They need a pride to survive. And so do you.*

=⚎=

WHEN THE SKY GREW DARK that evening, Stone Boy sized up a tree and grabbed Jack's hand. Jack scaled it in seconds. He'd never thought he could climb so well! He almost dropped the Bergen, but Stone Boy grabbed it and hooked it onto a forked branch. Like a trapeze artist, gripping the trunk with one hand and supporting Jack with one foot, Stone Boy secured himself, Jack, and the bag all at once, then seemed to dive back down— no, he was just hanging from his feet, plucking eggs out of nests in the branches below for their dinner.

Jack groped at the Bergen. The glass pieces were in it—he could feel their jagged edges through the tough elastic fabric.

In the morning, he thought, as the sun slipped behind the peaks of the inner rim, *I'll build a fire high enough to roast birds flying over!*

=⚎=

122

JACK'S DAD HAD ONCE told him about a game hunter in Africa who was also an expert in survival techniques. One day, just when a lion lunged at him, his rifle jammed.

The man found himself on his back, the lion pinning him down, its terrible fangs hovering over his face. Those huge incisors could decapitate a zebra in one chomp to the neck. One bite to that game hunter's face would have been the end of him.

The game hunter had to think fast. Using the only weapon he had, he smashed his fist into the lion's nose, as hard as he could, just to delay that first bite that would have taken off his face, and some of his brain with it. Then he stuck his right arm into the lion's throat.

Although the force of the lion's bite fractured his arm, the fist rammed into into its gullet made the lion gag and let go. The hunter rolled away, bleeding heavily. He reached for his bag, where he'd packed a handgun, and grabbed it with his left hand. Then he fired as the lion dove at him again. The bullet went straight through the lion's brain. One shot, and the lion was dead.

The game hunter tourniqueted his all-but-severed arm with his belt; then he called a rescue plane on his radio. The rescue plane found him wounded but alive.

Jack was dreaming that he was that game hunter, stalking a lion that could at any moment leap from the tall grass and kill him. In his mind's eye he made out the shape of the cat in the distance, body crouched low to the ground, eyes glowing, ready to pounce. *One shot*, Jack thought in the dream. *Make it count.*

He gasped and woke up.

The moon was bright, and the Bergen hung from a knot in the tree, right by Jack's nose. Stone Boy slept on a big branch in a seemingly impossible position: flat on his stomach, arms around the branch, with a foot shoved under Jack's chin, holding Jack upright as he slept. The back of Jack's head was against the tree, and his rear was wedged where the branch met the trunk. He was unable to move, and when he realized how high above the ground he was, he didn't want to. When he tried to free his throat, Stone Boy's foot instantly stretched out to reassert its grip. Jack tapped on Stone Boy's calf. Stone Boy didn't wake up. Jack eased the foot from his throat and laid it on his shoulder, while Stone Boy sighed as though he appreciated that less awkward position, and held Jack tight to the tree with spread-out toes.

Jack remained awake for a while. He stared into the night, feeling that his eyesight had changed. He could perceive so much more luminosity now, as if his eyes were adjusting to a world without electricity, neon, or car lights. Sounds seemed more vivid too: leaves rustling, wings flapping. Roars and calls. Even the silence sounded different, he thought. It had various degrees of quietness. Right before dawn, when the savanna clung to its last sleep, the silence seemed to peak. As soon as the sun rose, birds cawing, zebras whinnying, hooves thumping, and bugs zipping through the air turned the savanna into a huge soundscape, busy and humming with life.

Jack felt he was truly seeing and hearing for the first time.

I guess I'm getting more like you, Stone Boy, he thought. And he smiled, drifting off to sleep.

=‖=

He woke up blinking from the sunlight. He was alone in the tree. The sun was already high in the sky, illuminating the ravine below. The older lioness was creeping back from the acacia grove with an inert cub in her fangs. She spat him onto the ground, dead. Two males stepped up, bit the cub in two, and started eating it. The lioness turned and limped back up the ravine.

As Jack sat up and rolled his stiff neck, she returned with another cub in her mouth. All three lions listened intently, but there was no sound coming from up the ravine: The pride had not noticed the cubs' absence. The traitor lioness set down the second dead cub. The males devoured it, then let the lioness scavenge the innards. Jack watched, transfixed by the scene.

Suddenly, he started. The Bergen should have been hanging in front of his face, where Stone Boy had hooked it when they went up the tree. But it was gone. Perched on the high branch, he squirmed and felt bark against his feet. He was barefoot. Stone Boy had peeled his boots off his feet!

Jack looked at the ground, where Stone Boy

was hunkered down, biting and pulling at the Bergen. The fabric was so tough, he couldn't tear it, so finally he gave up, flinging the bag away. He jumped up and moved his feet rapidly, trampling on something. Then he grabbed a stone and banged it on the ground, where it made a clinking noise.

The glass, *the fire-making glass!*

"Stop it! Stop it!" Jack yelled, tumbling down from the tree. Stone Boy was trampling on Jack's boots, which were totally flattened and broken down now. The dictionary lay on the grass, partially destroyed. Jack stepped on tiny glass bits but didn't even feel them cutting his feet. Stone Boy heard Jack and turned just as Jack punched him, catching him squarely on the chin. He shoved Stone Boy to the ground and dove down, desperate to salvage what he could. *No glass, no fire, no way to signal to a rescue plane!* Jack grabbed the Bergen and threw it at Stone Boy's face.

"Why?" he yelled.

"Ua-ah . . ." Stone Boy imitated him, and then he kicked Jack to the ground. He stared at Jack, stunned. And then his face changed from an expression of innocent curiosity to one of worry.

Jack got up on one knee and touched his face, muddy now from dust and tears. He howled at Stone Boy: "This is all I have!" Jack grabbed the knife and the broken glass and stuffed them into the Bergen. He picked up the boots and hurled them into the distance. They were useless now. "How am I going to get out of here without boots? What am I going to do now? I don't know why I thought you could help me. You're no better than a baboon!" he yelled furiously, tears running down his cheeks. He had to get out of there, away from Stone Boy.

=⫲=

JACK RAN, slowing at the edge of the ravine.

He looked across, at the ravine's opposite bank, and saw the limping female and the male lions. She had stolen and killed another cub. One lion shoveled dirt over the carcass, scratching with his hind paws like a cat in a litter box. Then he sniffed what he had buried, as if to be sure he had hidden it well. Jack was glad the lions had just eaten. They wouldn't be hungry for a while.

Striped gazelles hurried up the bank, nervously

monitoring the lions. There were so many . . . Jack's anger at Stone Boy surged again. "You idiot," he mumbled aloud. "We could've hunted together! We could be having gazelle for dinner tonight."

He dropped down onto a crag and sifted through the broken glass in his Bergen, finding two pieces barely larger than postage stamps. But they were rounded like magnifying glasses, having covered some gauges on the plane's instrument panel.

He plucked some dry grass off a rock and piled it on the ground. Then he held one chip of glass above the other, focusing a beam of sunlight onto the grass, which started to smolder. A curl of smoke rose and thickened, a red core taking form at the center of the pile.

He had a flame.

"All right!" Jack hollered, and pumped his fists in the air. "It worked! I did it!"

Jack stared at the flame, and at his hands, which had built a fire for the first time. The fire's success turned everything into a promise, and Jack suddenly grew confident that his body would carry him through whatever lay ahead, boots or no boots. The soles of his feet had already begun to develop calluses from running hard and jumping and climbing. They were almost bush-proof already; if he was going to trek out of here, his feet would be the least of his worries.

He grabbed the knife, started sharpening its blade against a rock.

The little fire, unfed, gave out. But Jack grinned. He could make another one.

=‖=

WHEN JACK RETURNED to the tree he had slept in, Stone Boy was nowhere to be seen. Jack sighed in relief and picked up the dictionary lying in the grass. He decided to hang on to it: The paper might be good for starting fires.

He looked up to the tree, half hoping to see Stone Boy.

The afternoon was still bright, but soon, he knew, twilight would chase the herbivores toward sparse bush. They preferred thinner vegetation for the night, short grass, where lions could not hide easily. Jack felt that he understood the bush so well now. *Who says I can't hunt an antelope on my own?* he asked himself. He was still angry at Stone Boy, though he had to admit that he missed him.

"Too bad," he muttered. "You might have been in for a real treat: antelope steaks, well done."

＝‖＝

THEN HE HEARD the clamor of the lions again, down in the ravine.

He realized he'd left the glass chips on the cliff. He stuck the dictionary in his belt and sprinted back, knife in hand. When he reached the cliff, he saw the pride from the acacia grove, half a dozen lionesses at least, closing in on those marauding males. Apparently they had finally figured out where to look for their missing children, and now they marched, tails to the ground, down into the ravine. A few of them held the last surviving cubs in their jaws.

Downwind, the two rogue lions flattened themselves to the ground and waited.

Unexpectedly, the turncoat lioness sprang in front of her sisters, as if to signal that the ravine was safe. The lionesses continued to advance until they stepped right into the trap: The lions leaped up fiercely, and the tangle of bodies went down in a cloud of dust. Jack spotted the chips of glass, dashed in to grab them, and scrambled back up the bank.

Then he saw Stone Boy on the opposite bank: He had taken cover behind a meager clump of grass and was digging with his feet, trying to make his hiding place deeper. As the lions tussled, Stone Boy huddled low, while from the grass and the groves on both sides of the ravine hyenas and wild dogs came at a run, panting excitedly. The entire savanna seemed to be in upheaval over the lions' battle. Several hulking baboons slunk down the cliff and dropped into the ravine. Jack froze. Those baboons were so huge, he'd never seen any like them before. After assessing the conflict, they sidled off. Then Stone Boy inched his head up, raised one arm above the grass tops, and waved at Jack. Jack hesitated, then waved back. Stone Boy broke into a dead run down the bank, his stride long, indistinguishable from a human's. He crossed the ravine just a few yards from the fighting lions, pulled himself up over the edge, and stood sheepishly before Jack.

Then he bent down and scooped a handful of dust off the ground, found an atom of glass in it, and held it out to Jack: Here. He made a plaintive sound: *Ua-ah.*

"It's all right," Jack muttered, picking up the tiny piece, accepting the apology.

Stone Boy nodded and bent his knees, making his body small as if to acknowledge Jack's dominance, but what he was really communicating, Jack guessed, was not about dominance or submission. Jack remembered that Dad had shown him documentaries of Jane Goodall's research about chimpanzees. The chimps could communicate with the humans, and now Jack could see that a hominid could do that just as well, or better. Stone Boy was signaling that he was wrong to destroy Jack's things, and a lot more than that. Stone Boy had been communicating with Jack ever since he'd wrapped Jack's arm with mud and ants, and let the ants' fiery bites stitch up Jack's wound. Even then, his eyes, his gestures, had conveyed messages. Stone Boy had protected Jack and sought his trust from day one. What a gift it was to have an ally in a place like this. *Together*, Jack thought, *we can make it out of here.*

Stone Boy straightened up, as if to say: Time to move on.

"Wait," Jack said.

He turned to a tree and tore off a low branch. Stone Boy watched Jack's handiwork with focused attention. Intrigued, and perhaps already learning. Jack stripped one end of the branch, making it almost into a spear tip.

"It's not a spear yet," Jack said. "But it will do for now."

Stone Boy's gaze was so attentive, yet so vulnerable and intimate too. Jack imagined Stone Boy as an infant, tumbling around with others like him, his tribe, a little creature with stiff hair who swung in trees and yet walked surefootedly. Look how he seemed to be learning just now; he must have learned to throw hunting stones from other siblings or parents. Where was his tribe?

Stone Boy put his long hand on Jack's as if urging him: *Come on, follow me.*

They started back toward the ravine, crouching to the ground near the edge. Peering over, they saw that the older lion had just killed one lioness. He still held her lifeless neck in his jaws. The other lionesses jumped on his back, trying to free their sister, but it was useless. The traitor lioness was busy chasing the last two surviving cubs. She lunged and bit their hind legs, disabling them one at a time. The rogue males would do the rest. The dead lioness fell from the lion's jaws and lay motionless on the ground. *That could be me*, Jack thought. *That is me, if I don't make it out of here soon.* He felt like getting up and sprinting, not stopping until he crossed over the rim.

In the ravine, a young mother, now childless, attacked the traitor lioness. They went down in a ball of bodies, biting, scratching. The males entered the fray and pinned the bereaved mother to the ground. The mother rolled onto her back submissively, and the two males let her live. Then the males herded the females away, down the slope.

As the lions escorted their conquered pride, a pack of cackling hyenas poured into the ravine. They'd watched the rumble from the banks and were ready to feast on the dead lioness. But when they spotted the two bipeds, they moved to encircle them, competition for a fresh kill. Stone Boy tugged Jack's arm, pulling him after the departing lions. Jack held back, trying to consider his options. *Come on*, Stone Boy's anguished face pleaded, *we must follow the lions!*

He's right, Jack thought in amazement. *The lions are busy now forming a new pride, and they hunt only every four or five days. In between, they sleep. Just now, if we're careful, they're less danger than the hyenas! Yes, we'd be safer diving into the ravine and following the lions. . . .*

They were standing at the edge of the bank, practically surrounded. A snarling hyena lunged at Jack. He deflected it with his Bergen.

One shot, he thought.

With a guttural yell, Jack shoved Stone Boy off the bank. They jumped.

CHAPTER TWO

Jack and Stone Boy walked behind the lions for hours at a safe distance, yet never losing sight of them. The lionesses walked one behind the other in single file, apparently resigned to their fate. The males patrolled the flanks of their marching column.

Jack was exhausted. His thoughts drifted.

He reflected that lions' social structure and behavior was amazingly complex. The lionesses cooperated in a pride and showed compassion for their young. Their behavior protected existing genetic lines. The males, on the other hand, brutally ended existing genetic lines, starting new ones to carry on their own genes. But both strategies had the same final goal: to ensure the lion's ultimate survival as a species.

Jack had once asked his father what made human beings human: Was it articulate speech, or walking erect, or using tools, or living socially? Which single factor more than all the others allowed humans to advance beyond every other species to the top of the food chain?

Jack's father had reflected for a moment before answering. "All those factors, of course, play a role. But I think what makes us truly unique is our ability to be both cooperative and aggressive, to go from one to the other so swiftly and easily. What humans seemed to realize from the very beginning was that both of these qualities are equally useful when it comes to survival."

"So violence and war actually help us survive?" Jack had asked.

"In terms of our individual survival, they can, yes," his father answered. "In terms of the survival of the species, I don't know. Many early human societies went extinct because of conflicts between tribes. If those early humans had cooperated better, they might still be around. Given how much war we've lived through as a species, it's a wonder that we're still here at all."

Marching behind Stone Boy, Jack thought: *I was ready to kill him when he broke that glass. But I didn't. I realized that we were better off together than alone. Dad was right.*

Around midday, a muddy little stream appeared at the bottom of the ravine. The lions stopped and drank at it. Jack was so thirsty, he bent down to drink, but the stream had been dirtied by the lions. He wondered how long he could wait before they found fresh water. The females kept moving, pushed along by the lions. Traitor began to lag; her leg wound had reopened during the fight. The males slowed down for her and, with brief basso roars, seemed to encourage her. *She must still be useful to them,* Jack thought in a daze. When night fell and the moon came up, Jack started to stumble, and Stone Boy helped him up several times.

"Thanks, Stone Boy," Jack muttered. "You're a good friend."

Stone Boy smiled in the darkness and pursed his lips as if telling him to be quiet.

They entered a wooded area. Groves and clusters of lush bushes everywhere promised that there was water nearby. The male lions walked around, spraying the grass and the tree trunks with their scents. Satisfied that their new pride base seemed safe, they roared softly, and the lionesses settled in.

Jack and Stone Boy discovered a brook and stole to the water, glancing worriedly at the pride. But even now the lions were busy. Traitor licked the males' faces, then walked over to her sisters. She tried to make the scent of the conquerors familiar to them by rubbing against them and nuzzling their ears. The females pulled back, a few of them snarled, but they were too exhausted to fight again, so Traitor went on, doing her part in cementing the new pride.

After drinking their fill, Jack and Stone Boy found a campsite in an acacia grove littered with broken tree trunks. Jack speculated that they had been uprooted by elephants.

Good for firewood, he thought, clutching the little pieces of glass in his pocket.

CHAPTER THREE

One afternoon a few days later Jack chose a tree to sleep in and prepared it as he had seen Stone Boy do several times: He scaled the trunk, tearing off any branches that stood in the way of a quick ascent, but kept a few critical handholds.

Jack's prepared tree looked only slightly different from the rest of the grove and if he straddled a branch near the top, he had a clear view of the ground below. Although it was unlikely that a leopard would venture so close to the lions, if one tried to climb the tree, Jack would be able to see it well in advance.

As he tore one last branch off, he felt the muscles in his arms flex beneath his taut skin. By now he was visibly thinner, but his body was becoming stronger, more muscular, like Stone Boy's. He piled some of the branches next to him on his perch— spears to nudge birds and monkeys out of the tree—before settling in for the night. Stone Boy sat on the ground, holding one precious chunk of glass over another above a clump of dry grass, angling them to catch a ray of sunlight. Jack realized Stone Boy must have been watching him before, when he had started a fire on the rock overlooking the ravine. He was amazed that Stone Boy had learned from him so quickly. When a beam of light finally hit the glass, Stone Boy chirped excitedly, pleased with accomplishing this first step.

"Here," Jack said, dropping from the tree and picking up the glass pieces. "Try this." He sat beside Stone Boy and held the glass pieces in front of him. "If you hold them above each other and let a sun ray go through both, you double your odds of starting a fire. Like this." He held the two shards of glass above each other. Stone Boy snatched them from him and showed him again how, by holding them away from each other, he could catch a sun ray in each. Patiently, Jack took the two pieces and held them above each other . . . and suddenly, a sun ray piercing through the canopy above them made both pieces of glass glow at the same time.

Stone Boy took the glass pieces and tried to hold them just as Jack had. And the sun ray found its path through the air and through the two layers of glass.

"That's right, that's it!" Jack whooped.

He clutched the little hominid's wrists to hold Stone Boy's hands at that angle, so he wouldn't lose the sun ray, as the dry grass started to smolder and caught fire under the glass.

"You're good at this," Jack said.

Stone Boy was used to Jack's voice now. Most times he didn't glance up when Jack talked. But now he heard the excitement in Jack's voice, so he stared back and softly growled that *ua-ah* sound, which had become a kind of special reply. Stone Boy uttered it only at certain times, when they sat together as they did now, whittling a spear, or playing with the sun rays till the grass kindled.

Suddenly they heard rustling in the grass and froze. Stone Boy looked at Jack, his eyes wide. Lion approaching. But it wasn't a lion on the hunt. Jack could see it was the same one who had taken on the traitor lioness and lost. She loped weakly toward him.

Jack ran to a pile of stones, lifted one, and pulled out a dead mole.

"Here, Girl," he called. "Come and get it!"

He held up the mole, then laid it on the ground and withdrew.

Girl came closer, nudged the mole with her nose, but didn't pick it up. In her eyes Jack saw loneliness and pain.

"Give up, Girl," Jack muttered. "Go back to your sisters." He took a step toward the lioness, who crouched for a moment and then retreated to the grassland, tail hanging limply. Jack followed her to the edge of the grove, the border between the boys and the beasts.

He could see the pride in the distance. The males nuzzled two females, who no longer resisted them. No doubt the lions would soon mate with the females, ensuring that the next generation of off-spring carried their genes.

"Another week and she'll be eating out of our hands," Jack said.

Stone Boy nodded, acknowledging Jack's relaxed and reassuring tone of voice.

Peering under the canopy, Jack glanced at the far sky, which looked so empty.

Maybe I've missed that plane forever, he thought. Despite feeling sad, he felt proud too. He had survived. Here he was, making fire, with his partner.

Crouching, Jack lowered his palms and tried to signal to Stone Boy: *patience*. He knew Stone Boy could be patient about many things—but not, apparently, about fire.

Jack pushed more grass into the flame, then piled on a few dry, broken branches. Stone Boy reached over to a little mound of dirt and dug out two spears they had whittled into sharp points. Monkeys might dash out of the trees to steal the spears and chew them to pieces, so the boys had buried them. They each took a spear and held it in the fire, sharpening the tips by charring them and then scraping the points on a rock.

Jack noticed that Stone Boy had lost interest in his throwing stones, which lay by a tree in a cluster. He hadn't used them for a few days, although he still tucked them in his armpits when they traveled. Now he grinned at Jack, stoking the burning branches with his new favorite weapon. The end snapped off and fell into the flames, but Stone Boy quickly repaired it.

"Now it's too short. That's enough," Jack said, gently taking the spear from Stone Boy's hands, heat from the charred tip moving up along the lean branch to Jack's fingers. The spear felt alive.

He handed it back to Stone Boy, who ran his long finger along its side, gazing at his creation admiringly. It was straight, narrow, and sharp—a combination of shapes that did not appear naturally in the bush. Stone Boy looked at the spear unafraid, the same way he looked at the fire. He seemed to understand that he had power over the flames, if not to make them, then at least to maintain them. When the fire began to die down, Stone Boy leaned over and blew on it, as he had watched Jack do earlier. Flames popped up and rose above the brush and branches.

"Good! That's it!" Jack said, smiling. Stone Boy, looking triumphant, leaped to his feet and, throwing his shoulders back, broke into a joyful run. Jack caught up with him, and they sprinted to the edge of the ravine.

The side of the ravine was treeless but covered in grass that attracted herds of reedbucks and klipspringers. The ledges were difficult to reach, but the herbivores had figured out a way to access them, climbing from rocky outcrop to rocky outcrop much like mountain goats.

Holding their spears at their sides, the boys crept toward the animals, trying to move as stealthily as possible. The reedbucks looked as if they could be four feet at the shoulder, and the kudus grazing among them were even taller. Sensing the presence of predators, the animals brayed and began to descend into the ravine, where they could dash away from danger.

Stone Boy launched his spear. He missed, but barely, and immediately threw a stone toward the herd, striking an animal on its haunch. The buck stumbled but kept running, and Stone Boy darted in to retrieve his spear.

Jack paused for a moment, trying to anticipate the direction of the herd. He took off after them, holding his spear high and squinting through the cloud of dust stirred up in the animals' wake. When he had a clear shot, he raised his arm to hurl the spear, but he slipped, flinging the weapon aimlessly.

The herd fled along the bank's edge, bolting left and right, splitting into smaller groups. The boys pursued them, retrieving and throwing their spears as they went. They drove the herd together again, and the animals pounded the ground as a swift mass of hooves. Jack watched his spear fly after the herd and fall several feet behind it. But he knew success was possible. Pieces of spears and remains of butchered herbivores had been discovered at prehistoric sites, along with bones of early humans.

When the herd split once more, Jack ran after one group and Stone Boy pursued the other. Both boys managed to come up alongside the animals, steering them back together. The reedbucks panicked as they turned inward, stampeding toward the middle and trampling one another.

Jack frantically ran alongside the herd, close enough to see the whites of their terrified eyes. He raised his spear above his head, fixed his eyes on a big male, and brought the spear down into the animal's side! But the reedbuck's hide was so tough, only a few inches of the spear could pierce it. Jack held on to the end of his weapon fiercely, lunging after the still-running animal, screaming. Stone Boy appeared beside him and stabbed the animal with his own spear. Jack withdrew his weapon and plunged it into the buck's neck. The buck fell, writhing as the hunters held fast. Within minutes, the buck was lifeless.

Stone Boy and Jack stood up, gasping and red-eyed from the dust.

They had done it. They looked at each other, connected by their sense of triumph. Jack's heart was beating so hard, he could feel it in every finger-tip. Still panting, he pulled out his knife and started carving a back leg.

Two other reedbucks had been gored during the stampede. A waste for the hunters, but not for the wild, Jack knew. Hyenas would be here in no time. The dead bucks were beautiful, their proud horns shining. This kill was for survival, he told himself. Stone Boy wrenched the knife from Jack's hand and carved the other leg, tearing more than carving. Looking up, Stone Boy laughed. *Now we eat.*

They returned to the acacia grove, each carrying a leg sticky with blood. The fire at the campsite had burned down to embers but was quickly revived when Jack fed it more dry grass and branches. When the flame grew hot enough, Jack laid the buck's legs across it. The animal's hair smelled as it singed; then the meat, catching fire, sizzled. The flames grew taller, catching bugs flying over the fire. Stone Boy stood on the other side of the flames, deeply entranced.

Jack closed his eyes and listened to the meat roasting. Then a puff of smoke blew into his face: Half of a leg had fallen into the fire. The brush stirred. Jack yanked the leg out but dropped it.

"Ow!" He blew on his burned fingertips.

Leaves and dirt were stuck to the meat. Once it had cooled enough to handle, Jack held it to the flames to burn the debris off and charred it black.

When he finally put the meat into his mouth, the world he had known before the plane crash reached out for him, and his memories of life back home surged forth so forcefully, he was almost overwhelmed.

He devoured the meat, thinking of the last time he'd spent with his dad in California, three years before. They'd spent warm summer nights grilling steaks on the barbecue—just the two of them. The memory was so strong, Jack almost felt his father was there beside him.

Jack swept his tears away with the back of his hand. Turning to Stone Boy, who was watching him eagerly, he said with false enthusiasm, "Well, come on! Chow down!"

Stone Boy picked up his piece, finding it so hot to the touch that he tossed it from one hand to the other until it cooled off. But once it had, he ate ravenously, smacking his lips.

Later, having gorged on the meat, Jack felt blissfully full. Stone Boy started a game of jumping over the fire. He waited for the flames to die down a little, then took a running start and leaped over the fire, hooting with laughter. Even when he burned his toes, he only yelped and leaped over the fire again. When Stone Boy had tired of his game, he tackled Jack, and the two tumbled beneath the trees like lion cubs.

For the first time since the plane crash, Jack didn't feel the dull ache of hunger. Bugs buzzed around them, attracted by the smell of the meat. He slapped the air with his hands, but the buzzing didn't stop. In fact, it only grew louder.

In the sky above the most distant peak of the Witch's Pot, something was moving. It was small and cross shaped, glinting in the sun as it circled.

An airplane.

CHAPTER FOUR

Jack ran into the grassland shouting, waving his arms at the tiny plane. He raced, screaming at the top of his lungs, oblivious of lions or anything else that might be lurking in the tall grass. "Hey! I'm here! I'm here!"

The plane quivered in the turbulent drafts that rocked the air above the peaks.

Although Jack knew there was no way the pilot could hear him, he yelled as loud as he could. His heartbeat pounded in his ears, almost louder than his voice.

"I made a fire!" Jack screamed, lunging with his whole being in the direction of the plane. He spun back toward the campsite: in front of him, a billow of black smoke bloomed above the trees.

The smoke, Jack thought. *He'll see the smoke.*

Stone Boy stood rapt at the treeline. He had seen the plane and was now frozen in place, connecting this strange object in the sky with that other strange object, the one that had crashed in flames. He squatted, almost blending into the grass, staring at Jack, who kept shouting and waving his arms: "Frank! Frank! Here I am!"

The plane completed a circle and, fighting strong winds, struggled to gain altitude. Jack ran to the edge of the ravine and fell to his knees.

"Frank! Look! I made a fire! Fraaa . . . aaa . . . aankk!"

Jack looked back to the acacia grove, where the smoke blew higher, hard black above green, perfectly visible in the sky. *He's got to see it, he's got to!* Jack thought frantically. The plane didn't have to march across the bush, traipse through a ravine, or climb trees. All it had to do was fly toward the smoke.

154

"Are you blind?" Jack shouted.

When it changed direction, the glitter of sunlight against the fuselage was so dazzling, Jack just stood there blinking.

And then there was no plane, only the sound of the engine, whining on a different pitch as the plane flew away from him.

He's just going behind that crest, Jack thought. *He'll come back!*

But the plane didn't return.

Jack walked back toward the campsite but stopped halfway across the field and threw up. Thoughts clamored inside his mind. All he'd learned about surviving in this place—how to walk, how to eat, how to make weapons and fire, how to work together with the creature who had saved him—one plane showed up and made it all worthless.

Then Stone Boy snapped out of his daze and ran to his friend. But the joy of the hunt and the thrill of the fire had gone out of his eyes. Instead, he seemed very frightened.

"It's okay, Stone Boy," Jack reassured his friend.

The little plane had managed to pierce through

the storms: It should be only a matter of time before a larger plane returned with a rescue party. At least now he knew where that rescue party would show up. Beginning to set, the sun shone brightly against the far rim, dead east. *I can make it there,* he thought. *I can walk that distance, no problem. And when a plane shows up again, I'll be right under it.*

Jack laughed weakly, giddy with the thought that rescue was just over the horizon. Stone Boy sat beside him, his eyes wide with worry. Jack reached out and touched his cheek. Stone Boy gave a start but didn't pull back. With his index finger Jack traced the wrinkle in Stone Boy's brow from one end to the other. Slowly Stone Boy reached out and gently pressed the bridge of Jack's nose.

"I'm going to meet that plane the next time it flies over," Jack said resolutely. "But what," he wondered aloud, "am I going to do with you?"

CHAPTER FIVE

Stone Boy sat beside the fire, wiggling his fingers and toes in the ashes around the edge. Jack sat facing him, sweat pearling on his forehead from the heat of the flames. He was reading aloud from the Swahili dictionary.

"Fire," Jack said in English, then looked at the translation. "*Moto.*"

Jack looked over at Stone Boy, who was inattentively fussing with some brush around the fire. "Listen," Jack said. "You and I are not that different. In a few thousand years, your kids' kids might pick this up—it's called reading, and it's pretty much going to change their lives. It's something only humans do, like wearing clothes."

He continued. English, then Swahili: "Firewood. *Kuni.* To set on fire. *Choma moto.*"

Jack wondered where *Homo sapiens* might be in a few thousand years. Sometime in the future a species that had gambled its fate on technological developments and weapons so much more powerful than spears might destroy itself. Only then, maybe, would Stone Boy's descendents get a fair chance to take over the Earth. They would come upon inscriptions in English and decipher them, like scientists had done with the Rosetta stone.

Stone Boy leaned toward Jack, peering over his shoulder at the book. His eyes glowed with unquenchable curiosity.

After being soaked by rain, the dictionary had dried stiffly, like parchment paper. Some pages stuck together. Jack separated them, pulling gently. Bits of grass were squashed onto the text. A wildflower, yellow, pollen rich, was preserved whole between two pages.

"We. *See-see.*"

Jack laughed and opened the book to the one entry that helped him stay sane. *"Hatawa,"* he said, staring Stone Boy in the eye. "It means action. And footsteps. *Pika hatawa*: Move ahead. *Chukua hatawa*: Take steps. You like reading?"

Stone Boy took the dictionary from Jack's hands. He lowered his forehead a little, just as Jack had done to read. Holding the dictionary on his lap, Stone Boy traced his fingertip up and down the page. A noise gurgled from his throat. *Eeee.* Jack laughed. Stone Boy grinned like a prankster and handed back the dictionary. Jack accepted it and set the book down carefully, away from the fire. He couldn't believe what he had just seen. Stone Boy understood that the images on the page and sound—language—were somehow connected. The thought was dizzying.

Jack recalled his first encounter with spoken Swahili, during that truck ride to the research center on his first day in Africa. Dad had taught him some Swahili names for animals: *simba*, lion; *kongoni*, wildebeest; *kiboko*, hippo; *kifaru*, rhino; *tembo*, elephant.

"What's man?" Jack had asked.

"*Mtoo*. And woman is *mwanamke*."

"*Mtoo?*"

Bruce, who had mentioned that his first language was Swahili, smiled. "You can also call a guy *mtoo* like you'd say 'dude' in English. And the names of the animals, some of them are based on sounds that the animals make. But *kiboko* and *kifaru*—hippo and rhino—start with *ki*, which means small."

"But they're not!" Jack had said.

"Early on," Bruce explained, "tribal people thought that words could tame an animal. By calling the rhino and hippo small, they tried to conquer their fear of such big animals."

Dad had joined in. "Swahili contains some incredibly old words, some maybe three thousand years old or more. Think about it, Jack. For thousands, maybe hundreds of thousands of years, the way we communicate has evolved along with us. Language is perhaps the most powerful tool we have to appease, to reassure, to subdue, and to cooperate."

Now, sitting next to the fire, Jack absorbed the gravity of that conversation, which felt like it had happened a lifetime ago. "What do you guys think about this?" he had said. "Maybe one day while hunting, one australopithecine hunter grunted at another: *'Mtoo!'* They didn't have language yet for 'Help me, this buffalo I speared just fell on me and I'm trapped,' so *mtoo* was just a noise, a call for help. Maybe other hunters came to rescue the first, and *mtoo* was so successful that, from then on, hunters used it to call to each other. It became the word for 'male hunter' and then, years later, just for 'male.' That could've happened, right?" he'd asked excitedly. Dad and Bruce had exchanged a glance and smiled.

"Maybe," Dad replied.

"Language probably *started* in the forest," Bruce had responded. "But it developed in the savanna, where prehumans needed to locate each other across much larger distances. So the more they used loud calls, the more specific those calls needed to be. That couldn't have happened in one day, Jack."

"But there had to be a first time for everything!" Jack had exclaimed.

"Jack, you just don't give up, do you?" Dad had said, smiling.

Jack had felt like hugging his dad just then.

I should have hugged him, Jack thought now, staring into the leaping flames. He unhooked the little metal clasp that opened the notepad attached to the dictionary's back cover.

There was only a hint of ink left in the cartridge of the ballpoint pen. Carefully Jack drew himself on the muddied pad as accurately as he could. He drew his feet in boots and his hair flopping over his ears.

Stone Boy bent over the page excitedly, his breath in brief, heaving bursts. Jack pointed to the boots in the drawing. "Look . . . boots." Then he pointed at his own feet, now bare. "My boots. This is me."

Jack drew a larger figure next to himself, then another one, to show Dad and Bruce. He added another figure, and drew breasts to show it was a woman.

He put his fingertip on himself in the drawing, and then pointed to his chest. "This is me. I'm here." Then he pointed at the other figures, and cast his arm out toward the savanna. "These are my friends, my family. They're out there."

He used what little ink was left to draw Stone Boy on a separate page. The wispy hair on his head was unmistakable, as were his long feet. Jack put his finger on Stone Boy's image. "This"—he pointed at Stone Boy's chest—"is you."

Then he searched Stone Boy's eyes, seeking some hint of recognition, of understanding. "Why are you alone, Stone Boy? Where is your family?"

Stone Boy was silent but seemed thoughtful. Jack turned a page and once again drew Stone Boy alone. Then he repeated pointing his finger at Stone Boy's chest, and back at the drawing. "Come on," Jack said. "I know you've seen your reflection before."

Stone Boy's eyes went from Jack to the drawing and back. He quickly licked the tip of his index finger and dabbed it in the ash. He pressed a gray smudge onto the page, to the right of his image, and then one to the left, then several more all over the page. Jack couldn't believe it. Not only did Stone Boy understand him, but he was drawing too.

"Family?" Jack asked. "You have family? All right. Now, where are they?"

He put his own finger onto Stone Boy's finger-prints, and then playacted with open arms, looking around. "Where are they?"

Stone Boy stared fixedly at Jack. Then he got up and walked off toward where the night wind made the grass ripple in a long wave.

So, Jack thought, *he understands the difference between alone and not alone, and one individual and many. But why is he alone?*

Jack's eyes itched from the smoke. He gathered the last kindling branches into a bundle and held them over the flames. They lit up at once. Holding the branches like a torch, he walked into the darkness after Stone Boy. He moved noisily, praying that the fire and the sound would scare off any creatures in his path. Bugs hovered above his torch, while nocturnal civets and mongooses escaped into the brush. When he lowered the torch, the ravine opened in front of him. He peered down and saw the pride, walking up the ravine, led by Girl. The two males tottered after Girl, and Traitor walked alongside the males, and all the other lionesses followed, tails up. Stone Boy crouched by the edge of the bank, watching. *I should put down the torch,* Jack thought. Suddenly, down below, Girl stopped. The old male stopped too and pawed the ground. Sniffing Girl, he scratched the dirt, summoning her to lie down, which she did, folding her legs beneath her.

Another female stepped forth from the pride and approached the younger lion, slapping his side with her tail. The two circled each other for a moment. Then, suddenly, Girl leaped up and was on Traitor in a split second, sinking her teeth into her enemy's neck. The other females pinned Traitor to the ground and ended her quickly. The scuffle was so short, the males had no time to react. The females' brutal efficiency was stunning. Girl sat back, her muzzle bloody and glistening under the full moon. The males paced about nervously, making no attempt to save Traitor. The lionesses stood together and faced them. Jack held his breath. Surely the lions would retaliate. But they didn't.

They're weak! Jack thought, astonished.

The females growled at the males and advanced toward them. Outnumbered, the males retreated, jogging up the bank and out of sight.

Stone Boy looked at Jack. Both of them were stunned, and yet something they had witnessed spelled the law of survival again, so clearly that all they could do was nod to each other. After losing their cubs, the females had had no choice but to accept their captors' genes. Which didn't mean that they had accepted them as permanent partners; that temporary acceptance had been purely opportunistic. The females wanted new offspring, and this was their only option to become mothers again. But those cub-eating males offered nothing protective or generous to the females, not even teamwork when the females hunted. The females did the hunting themselves, while the males relaxed and then helped themselves to the kills. The females had only one use for them: their strong, healthy genes. Now, after they had mated with them, they had used this last maneuver to punish Traitor and banish the males. . . . Staring at how the lionesses regrouped, solidary sisters again, Jack cried in pain: The torch had burned on while he watched, and had scorched his fingers. He dropped the last burning branches, kicked dirt over them, and nursed his burned fingers.

Stone Boy too had been staring at the pride. Jack's cry of pain made him bolt in alarm. "Eeeeeee!"

"Don't worry, it's just the torch. It's out now," Jack reassured him, but it wasn't the torch Stone Boy was afraid of. Having just frightened off the males, the lionesses were suddenly climbing the bank, with Girl at the forefront. Girl, who had come crawling to the boys sniffing for food, now led her sisters to the nearest moving prey—Stone Boy and Jack. The boys scrambled up a tree. Girl paced around the trunk, swishing her tail. Then, perhaps wearier than she appeared from ending Traitor, the lioness changed her mind. She led the females off into the bush to pursue easier prey.

Jack forced himself to breathe evenly. *Safe for now*, he thought, *but it won't be long before the lions return. And when they do, we need to be ready.*

CHAPTER SIX

Stone Boy slept fitfully by the fire, sweating from its heat. Jack couldn't fall asleep. Instead, he patrolled the campsite, collecting more dry branches and feeding them to the flames. His thoughts drifted to the pride's astonishing behavior and Stone Boy's reaction to it. Perhaps a battle for dominance, similar to the lions', had separated Stone Boy from his kin. He wondered if Stone Boy's tribe was hiding close by, but realized that they might not approach Stone Boy in Jack's presence. If they were nearby, Jack hoped they would observe him long enough to realize he wasn't a threat. Stone Boy was an incredible discovery, but witnessing a whole tribe of prehistoric humans in action would be unreal.

It was almost dawn now. In the morning, Jack decided, he would go hunting. Finding another herd of herbivores wouldn't take long, and once he did, he could easily chase a few of them off the edge of the ravine. He would be more efficient this time, instead of just taking a leg and leaving the rest of the animal for scavengers. Once he dragged his kill back to the fire, he would roast it as long as he could, until little moisture remained in the meat. This, Jack theorized, would make it kind of like jerky—portable, protected against spoiling, and full of nutrients.

With the jerky packed in his Bergen, Jack would hike to the volcano's rim. He would eat the meat slowly, a few little meals each day. That way he could budget his strength. He hoped the meat would last him all the way out of the crater. If it ran out, he would have to stop and hunt again.

Stone Boy stirred in his sleep. Jack wondered if the little hunter would follow him. *His place is here,* he thought. *We're such a great team, but he was doing fine without me. He'll be all right.*

Still, Jack worried, *what if Stone Boy is the last survivor of his breed? What if they've died out and he's alone? If that's the case, he might need help even more than I do.* Yet Jack knew he couldn't take Stone Boy with him. Civilization would destroy him. At the very least, the intense scrutiny and study he would be subjected to might be more than he could bear.

What would Dad do? Jack wondered, weighing the possibilities. *If I tell anyone about him, it will have to be someone I can trust, like Frank.*

But what if Frank had made it to that first rim but the plane never came back? What if they had called off the search? If the rescue team had discovered the wreckage, they might have assumed everyone on board had died in the crash. Jack's only choice, in that case, was to get out of the Witch's Pot on his own.

Before the sun rose fully, Jack made a new spear from a branch that was larger than he had chosen before. Its tip was very sharp, honed into a point from being repeatedly thrust into the fire. Jack was well rewarded for his efforts. The new spear was the heaviest he'd made yet. Although it would be harder to run with, it would be infinitely easier to take down his prey now.

With his task complete and the horizon growing gray, Jack slumped to the ground. He slept for a short while and awoke to a cool and cloudy day that hinted at rain. Up on the peaks, sheets of water poured down through dark clouds. If rain was headed his way, Jack thought, he'd have plenty of fresh water for his trek out.

As he stood up, Jack reached down and fastened his belt tightly around his waist, securing his cargo pants. The pants, which had at one time covered his ankles, now hung in shreds above his scraped kneecaps. When he sat down, they dragged up his thighs, baring muscles and peeling skin. As one sunburn healed, another followed, and Jack's skin grew darker.

Jack was lucky his pockets had survived. They'd become indispensable to him. In his right front pocket, he carried the knife and two chunks of glass, wrapped in a thick leaf so they wouldn't shatter if he fell on them. He'd buried other bits of glass at the campsite. His left pocket still held the dictionary, which was now down to a third of its original size and only vaguely rectangular. He'd also picked up one of Stone Boy's hunting stones and tucked it next to the dictionary.

Meanwhile, because he too carried more survival tools now, Stone Boy had devised a new method of transporting his belongings: a strand of vine tied around his waist. Two hairy objects hung from the vine: two lion's paws. While Jack slept after the pride's battle, Stone Boy had crept to Traitor's body at dawn and claimed her paws as his prize.

Stone Boy untied the paws and pressed them into the ground around the fire. It took Jack a moment to realize what he was doing: Stone Boy was trying to deceive other intruding lions.

Seeing the prints on the ground, lions would think that the territory was claimed by another pride, and if the fire hadn't already deterred them, they would leave the campsite alone. *Good trick,* Jack thought, impressed that Stone Boy had thought of the ruse first.

Thirsty, Jack found a crack in the rocks that was

filled with cloudy water and dunked his face into it. When he finished making tracks, Stone Boy joined him and dipped his face in the water too. The coat of grime on his cheeks and forehead began to wash off, while Stone Boy coughed and spat in displeasure before he finished cleaning.

Spears in hand, they walked over to a high cliff where the rich grass had already lured herds of early-morning grazers. Jack considered the best approach for a moment and then ran, screaming fearlessly, along the high ledge toward a cluster of klipspringers. Several animals ran madly to the edge, and then Jack couldn't see them anymore: They'd jumped off. One bold buck stood his ground against the approaching bipeds, digging his hooves in and bracing himself. A poor choice of survival, for Jack loosed his arm like a catapult and sent his spear flying.

He missed. The spear flew into the ravine.

Stone Boy threw his own spear, but it veered off target. Running at the buck, Stone Boy let loose a hunting howl that sounded a lot like Jack's, only higher in pitch. *Ahhhhaaaawwwaa!* The buck could have gored him with its horns, but the noise was so startling that the klipspringer bolted, leaping off the cliff into the void below.

As the rest of the herd fled down the ledges, Jack and Stone Boy dove onto their stomachs and peered over the edge of the cliff. Their prey lay in the grass, unmoving. They spotted Jack's spear lying beside the animal. The other spear must have snagged in the bushes.

I'm a hunter now, Jack thought. We *are hunters*.

After climbing down into the ravine, Jack and Stone Boy cut the buck's body into smaller pieces to carry back to the campsite later. Jack retrieved his spear and looked around for Stone Boy's. He didn't see it.

Jack paced around the dead klipspringer with his lips pursed. He noted the terrain, the location of this most recent prey, and the access paths. The ravine narrowed here, which made hunting game easier. Vultures wouldn't be able to spot the downed animals from above, and scavengers like hyenas and jackals preferred the open range.

Jack squatted down and felt the animal's tracks. The ground was dry. Good. Behind him, Stone Boy untied Traitor's front paws and pressed them into the earth by stepping on them. Gripping the paws between his toes to hold on, Stone Boy made a trail of decoy lion prints. The twisting path was so realistically laid, it was indistinguishable from one left by a big cat.

Stone Boy smiled and held the paws out to Jack, who reached down and tried to make his own trail of prints. But it was hard to gauge where one print should follow the next. Stone Boy took the paws back and pressed new prints into the earth, putting the correct amount of distance between the front and back paws to reflect a lion's stride. He added an extra toe on the front paw marks to mimic the lion's natural prints: five toes on the front paws, but only four on the hind paws.

He's so smart, Jack marveled. *I didn't even remember that, and I've spent hours reading about lions.*

As Jack cut the klipspringer into manageable pieces, he realized that his idea of hauling pounds of smoked meat to the rim of the Witch's Pot might be more difficult to execute than he'd initially thought. Storing and transporting the jerky would attract ants and small rodents who wouldn't be deterred by the lion prints. *I'll have to protect the meat somehow*, he thought. Scavengers always trailed hunters; it was the way of the savanna. Soon, Jack realized, the two of them would be trailed, lion prints or no. Marching to the rim undetected by predators might be impossible once they caught a whiff of the jerky. Even cooked meat was a dead giveaway. He might slip by unnoticed if he carried mungongo nuts, but it would be difficult to escape the attention of a pack of hyenas with a pocketful of klipspringer fillet.

He could of course try to consume as much meat as he could before he set out on his journey, but that wouldn't keep him from being hungry or weak as he traveled. Jack wondered what his ancient ancestors did when faced with this dilemma. Over the past few days he'd felt as if he had achieved the ability to see the world through their eyes. But still, a clear answer did not come to him.

Stone Boy finished the trail of phony lion prints and hung the paws on the vine around his waist like tools on a utility belt. Jack laughed at the sight. So this was the dawn of technology—spears and lion paws. Two giraffes crossed the ravine, one fluttering its blue tongue at the other as if mocking its mate. In the distance a baby elephant trumpeted a distress call. Jack could see it in the distance, stuck at the base of the cliff, unable to climb out of the ravine. The adult elephants heard the call and appeared at the top of the ledge. One of them descended carefully, trunk extended, until it reached the baby and led it up the cliff face. The calf followed happily, twirling its tail like a piglet.

Stone Boy took a piece of the klipspringer's loin meat and packed it into Jack's Bergen. Jack turned to help him pull another thick steak from the animal's side, and as he did, a heap of dirt rose up behind Stone Boy.

A lion, the older of the two marauders, shook off the dust and slunk forward. He was in bad shape. Streaks of dried blood colored his chest, nose, and face like camouflage. His eyes were sunken like a prizefighter's and his coat was draped with ants. *He's been playing dead!* Jack guessed. The lionesses must be nearby. From his studies of pride behavior, Jack knew that in this situation the lionesses would kill the male if they found him alone, so the lion had spent the night here motionless, covered in ants. Jack wondered for a moment where the younger lion was, but judging by the amount of blood on the dust-covered lion's fur, he guessed that the two males had fought and only this one had survived.

The lion began to creep up behind Stone Boy, who was obliviously at work butchering the klip-springer. Jack froze. At this range the lion could pounce on Stone Boy in an instant and tear him limb from limb. Or he might just as easily walk away. The lion seemed to hesitate.

Jack sprang from where he stood, spear in hand. Even though he was terrified, an unknown force compelled him forward. Jack only had one shot to save Stone Boy.

THE LION PREPARED to leap.

Jack charged ahead with a fierce war whoop. Stone Boy spun around just as the lion's jaws opened, but Jack's yell threw the animal off balance. Gripping his spear with both hands, Jack raised it and thrust it toward the lion's already bloodied chest. *One shot.* Jack braced himself against the hulking lion, so close to his face that his panting breath blew Jack's hair back. Stone Boy threw his body into Jack's side like a buttress to a tower—no spear, no stones, just the weight of their bodies against the lion's. The animal's weight cracked the spear, but as it did, the tip pierced the predator's chest.

A throbbing from inside the lion's beating heart ran across the shivering spear and into Jack's hands. He stabbed deeper with all his strength, the lion openmouthed above him. The lion fell sideways, and the spear broke like a matchstick. Jack tried to pull the weapon free but couldn't. He clung to the fractured wood desperately, shaking so hard that he bit his tongue. The lion swatted, but his paws moved blindly. He tried to roar but could manage only a subdued gurgle. Saliva and blood dripped from the lion's mouth, and his hind legs thrashed. The lion grew still, his eyes staring blankly.

Jack's hand was bleeding. At first he thought the lion had bitten him, but then he realized that blood had spurted from under his nails as he'd gripped the spear. Jack almost collapsed from exhaustion, but Stone Boy caught him. After helping his friend up, Stone Boy darted to the lion, kicked him, and kicked him again, to make sure he was dead.

Jack crouched beside the lion. With trembling fingers he pulled a tuft of fur on the belly. The lion didn't move. The tawny body was like a mirage, too incredible to be real, yet it was. Jack couldn't believe that only moments ago, the same animal had been about to end his friend.

I killed a lion, he thought.

Fingers shaking, he pulled the knife out of his pocket. Stone Boy jumped aside as though Jack were signaling some lingering danger.

"It's safe now," Jack reassured him. Stone Boy nodded, as if Jack's talking was proof that every-thing was indeed all right. Jack stuck the knife into the tan fur, making his mark.

"We killed a lion, Stone Boy. Can you believe it?" Jack said. They stood still for a moment and stared at the body.

A hyena scrambled down the cliff, its feet knocking pebbles down the incline. But it was quiet, as if holding its breath—no howling, no laughing. For an instant Jack foresaw it jumping on the lion, settling some old score. Hyenas eat every-thing. But with a quick supple motion, the hyena grabbed the dead klipspringer instead and pulled it up the cliff, climbing backward.

The two hunters watched, but neither of them reacted.

"Well," Jack said, glancing at Stone Boy, "I guess we can eat lion too."

Jack knelt in the dirt and raised the knife to the lion's shoulder. Stone Boy marveled at the sight: A boy not much larger than himself was claiming a lion for a meal.

Jack felt like cutting off the lion's ears, or his tufted tail, as talismans of magical powers. Stone Boy stood beside Jack, grinning.

"I can't believe it," Jack said, laughing, a charge of hope surging through him. He looked down the ravine and saw the lionesses moving away from them, growing smaller in the distance. *I can do any-thing now*, Jack thought. *Anything at all.*

CHAPTER SEVEN

That night, Jack and Stone Boy climbed a rock and sat beneath a vast sky. After the glory of their triumph, Jack wanted nothing more than to tilt his head back and contemplate the glittering, star-filled heavens. The beauty and clarity of the uninterrupted view was breathtaking. Jack raised a piece of lion meat to his mouth. As he ate, a fiery dot shot under the moon. The meteor descended in a straight line, burning off into nothingness.

Jack was trying not to stare at Stone Boy, but he couldn't help it. As the light from the shooting star flashed across his face, Stone Boy stared solemnly at the sky and sighed. Earlier, Jack realized, Stone Boy would not have had the patience to lie here and gaze at the sky. On previous nights, Stone Boy had been too vigilant of the lions to rest. But now he finally relaxed and turned to Jack with a peaceful expression on his face.

If only you could see this, Dad, Jack thought. He wondered what Dad would do in his situation—if he would be able to return to civilization and leave his greatest discovery behind.

For the first time, Jack felt like a man. Both he and Stone Boy had undergone a test of will that day, and they'd survived. But Jack had also acted selflessly, throwing himself into harm's way to save his friend's life. If he had hesitated for even a moment, he would have lost Stone Boy to the lion, and he would be alone now. But together, as a team, they had done something spectacular. Manhood, Jack realized, was not so much a matter of strength as it was a matter of doing the right thing instead of the easy thing.

Jack and Stone Boy would make a trail of lion prints around the fire tonight. Or maybe not. With an unfamiliar sense of pride, Jack wondered if they needed to. They had proven themselves smarter and stronger than the lions. What did they have to fear?

CHAPTER EIGHT

As dawn approached and the fire died down to smoldering embers, a shadow crept close to the campsite. A long-toed foot patted the ashes and a hand reached for the spear at Jack's side. It clamped four fingers around the wood, a short thumb not quite reaching the index finger.

Jack's eyes fluttered open to the choking weight of the spear on his throat. His view, however, was obscured by a wide, hairy head. Pungent breath knocked him back, and when he tried to jump up, hairy arms held his ankles down. He struggled free, punching the air, and realized he was surrounded by a troop of hulking beasts.

"Eeeeee!" Jack wailed in alarm, astonished when his captors mocked him, *"Eeeeeeeee!"* echoing his alarm call. One intruder struck Jack with his forearm, stunning him. Reeling from the blow, he saw that these creatures looked much like Stone Boy. They had the same raw humanness, but they were much larger. Older than Stone Boy, for sure. But despite their linebacker shoulders and thick arms, the skin of their faces showed blemishes and rashes.

They're teenagers, Jack realized. Teenagers with necks wider than their faces!

He yelled out, hoping now that his alien sounds would stall the hulks. "Over here! Help! Stone Boy!"

On the opposite side of the fire, a hulk twice Stone Boy's size tried to restrain him. But twisting and growling, he broke free and ran to Jack's side. Stone Boy landed a well-aimed punch to the head of the creature nearest Jack. Jack, seeing an opening, dashed to the cliff of the ravine. He stood at the edge and gauged the distance to the bottom, but it was too high. There was nothing to do but run. A mistake—the hulks quickly caught up with him. At close range they didn't have the leverage to punch, but as they hurtled toward Jack, they swung their thick forearms like baseball bats. When a creature with a mohawk struck and missed, Stone Boy drove his head into the attacker's stomach, shoving him over the edge and into the void. Crashing down, Mohawk wailed. Stone Boy turned to the others with a fierce look in his eyes. Arms and legs flailing, he charged straight at them. He issued a long *"Eeeeeeee!"* in Jack's direction, but Jack was unsure of its meaning—flee or stay and fight? Still tangling with the creatures, Stone Boy freed one arm and waved toward the trees.

Jack took off toward the acacia grove. His mind raced as he ran past giant lobelias and orchids. *Where am I going?*

Like a fierce tide, the pack gave chase. Behind Jack, Stone Boy shot up a tree. The hulks followed, and Stone Boy flew through the trees above Jack, swinging from branch to branch. With one arm outstretched, he pointed: *Up ahead!*

Jack ran furiously, lashed by branches and tangled in vines, with the hulks' foliage-shattering storm on his heels. Ahead, Stone Boy hung from a branch and threw leaves at Jack, screeching. Then the hulk with the mohawk pulled himself up over the ledge to face Stone Boy. Side by side, Jack saw, their faces had a striking similarity. Was this Stone Boy's brother?

Jack turned and plowed through the tall thicket. Unable to see above the grass, he panicked. Who knew what could be hiding in the field before him? Suddenly he stumbled on a branch and tripped. When he pulled himself up, he realized the branch was actually a bone. The hairs pricked up on the back of his neck. He was surrounded by bones. Several skeletons were propped against a tree trunk, and on one Jack saw a foot with toes like Stone Boy's. As he took in the sight, he saw skeletons all around him: a mass graveyard for Stone Boy's kin. But these skeletons were smaller than the hulks—

A gourd whizzed past his face, cracking against a tree. Mohawk! From the tree above Jack, the creature launched another gourd. Jack ducked.

One of the other hominid teens descended from the branches, followed by a scrappy scarred companion. Others hung poised to jump down, like a gang closing in.

Jack reached for his knife—gone! He'd lost it when he'd dashed across the thicket. Instead, he pulled a stone from his pocket and clenched it in his fist.

"Stop!" he yelled frantically. "Don't come any closer!" The hulks didn't move, but they didn't seem frightened either.

Still wearing the lion paws on the vine around his waist, Stone Boy swung down from a branch, gripping a stone. His face rippled with anger.

Outsmarting the lions was one thing, Jack thought. *But these guys are almost as smart as I am and at least twice as big!*

Jack's eyes darted between Stone Boy and the hulks, taking in the scene. Stone Boy sounded just like them, looked almost just like them. But as much as they were similar, Jack realized, Stone Boy was different: *Their hands are made to swing from branches. They can't make fists!* Jack observed. *But Stone Boy can.* What did it mean? Was it possible that in only a couple of years, Stone Boy's line had adapted, so that Stone Boy was born with hands that could more readily grip and throw stones?

Mohawk started toward Jack, but Stone Boy lunged and knocked him down. The pack descended on Stone Boy in one dark mass, howling and yelling. Stone Boy punched with a tight fist and kicked adeptly, hurling his strong legs into a hulk's chest and knocking the wind out of him. He cornered another one, who swatted at him, but Stone Boy unleashed his fury and kicked him again and again.

Jack turned and ran from the melee, vaulting as fast as he could through the tall grass. *Don't let them catch up with me*, he thought. *Go faster!* He was running back toward the ravine. In the distance he could see an open, treeless space where the cliff dropped off. He made up his mind. *I have to jump.*

Mohawk and another creature caught up to Jack. They reached for his heels, but he swung back and slammed his foot into Mohawk's groin. Stone Boy ran up and tripped the other one, then darted to Jack's side.

Jack gripped Stone Boy's arm. "We have to get out of here!"

The hulk Stone Boy had tripped struggled to his feet. Stone Boy dashed back and tackled him, throwing fists and feet at whatever he could strike. Just then a female cradling an infant to her chest crashed through the thicket. Her eyes were wide beneath her knotty hair. She bared her teeth and made a desperate, high-pitched noise. Jack froze. Here was the alpha—every tribe had one, and she was clearly it. She moved past him, toward Stone Boy and Mohawk. Another noise, an impatient, demanding bark, seemed to say, "Stop it, you two!" Stone Boy saw her and pulled back, but not before the female struck him hard, flinging him to the ground.

Another female appeared from the thicket and rushed over. She had gaunt cheeks and long hair, and also held an infant tucked beneath her chin. The alpha female handed her baby to the long-haired one. She barked once more, and the marauding hulks, like unruly older brothers, leaped down from the trees. Meanwhile, younger females emerged from the thicket: the girls of the tribe. The males rushed at them, and the girls dropped the food they'd been foraging—nuts, roots, and tubers. Mohawk dove for a mungongo nut. The girls howled when they spotted the outsider, their eyes shuttling from Stone Boy to the human intruder, panicked.

Despite being terrified of her, Jack stared at the alpha female's face. Between Stone Boy and Mohawk the resemblance was unmistakable. Jack was looking at a family reunion. The alpha had to be Stone Boy's mother. Jack scanned the tribe. The figures before him were very different from one another—some of their bodies stocky, others slender, some with angular, hairless faces and others with more squarish skulls. Yet they were all so obviously related. It was as if in this last sanctuary of antiquity, the tribe, perhaps sensing its own vulnerability, had undergone an evolutionary explosion.

The alpha female sniffed Stone Boy and the stranger. She glanced at the lion paws at Stone Boy's waist, then grabbed him by the vine and marched him over to a tree. There, she spanked him while he squealed in pain. Jack stepped toward them, but when the alpha glowered at him, he shrank back. And since the alpha female hadn't killed him already, he decided he'd probably be safer if he didn't try to flee. The hulks would no doubt give chase if he did, and with Stone Boy occupied, Jack wouldn't be as capable of defending himself.

Stone Boy grimaced as he took his mother's blows. Finally he punched her back, into her open palm. She cried out indignantly and stepped back. The girls clung to one another, looking at Stone Boy sympathetically.

Still chewing the food they'd taken from the females, the hulks were grinning, pleased to see Stone Boy's punishment. Mohawk took a chance and lunged in to kick him. Stone Boy howled. The alpha grabbed Mohawk, and at once the whole gang sprang on her. Stone Boy bolted up protectively and they stopped. Mohawk growled. Jack's heart was pounding: In the blink of an eye, the balance of power could shift. If a son would beat—even kill— his mother, what kind of violent chaos would follow?

For a moment the tension was unbearable. Then the females rushed over screaming, and one of them pushed Mohawk aside, grunting reproach-fully. Mohawk snarled and slunk back into the shadows. The alpha female grabbed Stone Boy but didn't hit him. Instead she drew him close to her, and her face contorted in anguish. For several moments she wept without tears. *She must have missed him*, Jack thought. Stone Boy squirmed and tried to free himself, but she wouldn't let go. Visibly embarrassed, he glared at the girls, who looked on and giggled.

Meanwhile, Jack spotted a hunched figure limping between the trees. His shoulders were stooped, and a big scar stretched above one knee. But the creature's body was withered and weak, his eyes lost in gaunt sockets. When he turned, Jack could see that one side of his head had a deep wound that exposed the cranium. The face looked strikingly like Stone Boy's. Was he the father?

The outcast thumped toward the tribe, peering over the thicket but not daring to join them. He looked at Jack curiously. When Jack stared back at him, he cowered and hobbled away.

Maybe, Jack pondered, *he's the only survivor of whatever massacre left all those bones back there.* Jack thought back to his father's lesson about conflict and war. But what did the tribe have to fight over? They had plenty of space and ample food. So what was it?

The lions! Jack thought. Like them, the hominids must have battled over breeding rights—whose genes would survive and whose genetic material would, by default, die out. And in this war, if the size of the skeletons was any indicator, brawn had definitely won out over brains.

The alpha female ambled over to Jack and put her face very close to his. She sniffed him and bared her teeth menacingly.

Will she kill me now that Stone Boy is safely back with the tribe? Jack wondered.

Suddenly the tribe closed in on him. Jack could think of only one thing to do. He took a deep breath and made the noises he had heard Stone Boy make, chirps and twitters, hums and clicks. The female, taken aback, moved away from Jack's face, appearing to reconsider him. Jack dove for Stone Boy's waist, snatching the lion paws from the vine belt.

As Stone Boy watched, Jack threw them to the ground, placed his hands over them, and began to make a trail of lion prints. He had to tell them the story. He would make them understand.

CHAPTER NINE

With a halting growl, Stone Boy leaped into Jack's path and took back the paws. At first Jack thought his friend had turned against him. But Stone Boy knelt down, placed the paws on the ground, and began to make the tracks himself.

The apes sat rapt, watching Stone Boy, while Jack looked around, trying to find a branch he could break into a spear. He spotted one nearby and tore it from a tree.

Stone Boy set the stage by slashing the air with his arms, creating a sense of wide-open plain. Then he sprang his fingers in random directions, like savanna bushes breaking the flatness: here, there. He made the *zzzzzzzzz* of bugs flying, his audience chirping approval of his excellent imitation.

Stone Boy imitated kudus and klipspringers, holding two fingers up to his head as horns, then mimicked the placid expression of a grazing herbivore. Then Stone Boy snarled *rrrr-huh, rrrr-huh.* Lions. He picked up the paws and walked them, softly and stealthily, toward his audience.

From the youngest of the girls to the rowdy boys, everyone was frozen in suspense. Alpha narrowed her eyes as if she recognized the beast. Stone Boy changed his stance from moving gracefully to a cautious crouch. Just then, a large bug flew past his nose, so he instantly put it in the story, pointing high into the sky and making a *buzzzzz* not unlike the engine of a plane. With his index finger, Stone Boy traced a zigzag path down to the ground, and his arms flew out to signify a great explosion.

Then Jack saw himself through Stone Boy's imitation: upright and heavy-footed. Stone Boy tilted his forehead forward and walked flat-footed. The youngsters of the tribe were confused at first, but then the older females turned toward Jack, tittering. *Yes, this is him, the stranger Stone Boy brought with him.* The youngsters approached Jack smiling, poking at his feet, at his chest and back. They laughed. Stone Boy scurried over to Jack and touched the bridge of Jack's nose.

Jack was amazed at the complexity of Stone Boy's tale, at the skill with which he demonstrated setting, characters, and action. His gestures—shrugging, frowning, smiling, puckering the lips—all meant something. Jack's chest was heaving with fear and excitement. The tribe was clearly curious, but he was still unsure of his fate among these creatures, so brutally and unpredictably prone to violence. Evidence of their bloody feud was only a short distance away. What guarantee did Jack have that they wouldn't turn against him too?

But Stone Boy was now an outsider as well. Perhaps he had fled to the grassland during the battle to find safety. Perhaps he was the first of his kin to survive on the savanna.

Stone Boy completed a long and twisting track and then growled a lion's roar. His kin recognized the sound immediately—the girls bolted, and the older females stiffened.

Stone Boy stood on one foot, scratching a spot behind his knee, grinning proudly at the trail. Jack recognized the scene unfolding before him. Stone Boy pantomimed spearing the klipspringer and using the knife to cut up the meat. He looked so pleased with himself, *he had no idea that a lion was sneaking up behind him.*

Stone Boy held up the lion paws and roared, then motioned to Jack, summoning him to the stage. Jack rushed forward with the branch in his hands. He screamed and stabbed the branch at the lion paws. He stabbed hard and gripped the branch tightly. Stone Boy dropped the paws, ran to Jack's side, and threw his body against Jack's. The two of them screamed and held the spear up, as the invisible lion impaled himself.

Stone Boy made a last, weakened roar, gurgled, and fell to the ground. His foot twitched—the lion's tail slapping the ground one last time.

Their audience was silent, awestruck. Exhausted, Jack and Stone Boy sat on the forest floor. Jack made joyful sounds, rapid chirps and clicks, a pure release of nervous energy.

After a few moments of recovering from the excitement, most of the tribe stretched and relaxed as though after a large meal. But not Mohawk's gang. They lingered at the rear of the group, vigilant and rigid. Mohawk's wary eyes furtively assessed his tribe's reaction. He looked displeased that they had responded so enthusiastically to Jack and Stone Boy's play. The largest gang member in the tribe knuckle-walked away from the group and vanished into the thicket.

Jack understood the situation. The closer he and Stone Boy allied themselves with the alpha female and her followers, the more they threatened Mohawk and his crew. If Alpha favored Stone Boy over Mohawk, if she gave the smaller of the two apes more attention and food, Mohawk would not just stand by and watch. But one thought echoed in Jack's mind: *I'll do what I have to do.* They'd had one shot to prove themselves to the tribe, and they'd done it, incredibly, and as a team. *If Mohawk thinks he can frighten me now*, Jack thought, *he has a few things to learn. I am a hunter. I survive.*

CHAPTER TEN

Several days had passed since Jack and Stone Boy had joined the tribe. The forest was thick and tangled, sunless and skyless. Wherever Jack looked, the horizon was obscured by foliage. The air was damp; even the forest breeze felt stale.

Jack had a different sense of time than he'd had on the savanna. The day's own seasons—the optimism of morning, the laziness of midday, and the suspense of twilight—didn't really exist here. Time blended into one murky shade, alternating with darkness.

The young hominids were fascinated by Jack. At first they were tentative, prodding their hard fingers into his strange, hairless hands and face. They wanted to know just how like them he was. They examined Jack's chest, shoulders, and knees. They flipped him over and pulled at his limbs. When they started to tickle his feet, Jack worried he would die laughing but was surprised to feel almost no sensation—his feet had become callused during his time in the wild. The hominids were endlessly curious. Alpha joined in to assess the quality of Jack's skin. When she scratched him hard enough to draw blood, Jack pinched her arm hard. She yelped—but withdrew and let him be.

Half hidden in the branches of a large tree, Mohawk watched the scene. His gang pelted Jack with tiny rocks from above, but, stock-still and silent, Mohawk just observed. The pebbles stung, and when Jack finally jumped up and yelled "Enough!" the gang hustled off into the woods. Imitating their language, he had learned, was not nearly as effective as using his own. "Stop messing with me!"

The females froze and stared at him blankly, in

shock. The toy had rebelled—now what? Stone Boy snuck behind Jack and tore the filthy dictionary from his back pocket. He knew he could distract the tribe from Jack's body by opening the little book. The pages fluttered in the breeze. The book was alive.

Stone Boy looked at Jack and then back at the audience. "Good!" Jack urged him. "Talking distracts them."

And then, as naturally as though he had been doing it for years, Stone Boy replied. The sound didn't sound like "good." There was no audible *g* or *d* in it. Just the middle sound—the *oo*.

Close enough. The tribe gaped in amazement.

Jack was floored. "Perfect! That's wonderful!"

Stone Boy smacked his lips, blurting out the *p* and repeating it: "Pa-pa-pa-pa-pa."

"Excellent!"

Stone Boy brandished the little book for all to see. The tribe looked up in reverence, and then, just like that, the dictionary came apart. Jack couldn't believe his eyes. The spine tore, and what was left of the pad fell out.

Mohawk dropped down from the tree, grabbed

the dictionary, and retreated back into the foliage. Stone Boy moved to chase him, but Jack snapped, "No!" His friend looked frustrated but sat down anyway.

Chewed-up pages drifted down from the canopy. The other hominids rushed to grab them and tore whatever they could get their hands on to pieces. One female shredded a page with her nails, then used her spit to glue the pieces into her hair.

What remained of the meat he had stashed in the Bergen had by now gone bad. Weak and exhausted from hunger, Jack approached Alpha. "Food," he said, gesturing to his mouth. "Give me something to eat." He motioned toward his gaunt stomach, which grumbled as if on cue.

Recognizing his plight, Alpha pulled him to a tree and hoisted him up to a low branch. Jack panicked that she might try to nurse him, but instead she pulled a cluster of nuts within his reach. She kept watch while he ate, eyeing the spot where Mohawk's gang had retreated in case they rushed back and tried to steal Jack's meal. Stone Boy joined them, and they ate together until Jack felt full and clearheaded. For the first time in several days, he felt like he could focus on his mission of escaping from the Witch's Pot. He couldn't orient himself at all under the thick canopy, where the sun was only briefly visible.

What if I never find my way back? he thought. *I have to leave them, or risk going deeper and deeper into the forest. I have to find my way back by the sun.*

When the trio dropped to the ground, the tribe was foraging. Stone Boy stayed close to his mother, speaking to her in agitated sounds. She seemed to listen, and then other mothers joined them and Stone Boy seemed to make a kind of closing argument. Alpha grunted to the other mothers, who scratched themselves, apparently perplexed.

Jack watched them, made his decision, and got to his feet. "Well, it's been fun. But I have to get back now." Jack started off into the woods, but Stone Boy caught up with him in the blink of an eye and blocked his way. The mothers trooped up and encircled them.

"All right, jump me now. Go ahead," Jack replied.

Alpha sidled up to Jack, spat out some chew from the nuts they'd eaten earlier. She held it up to Jack's lips. Jack shook his head. She wiped the mash onto a sapling. Jack realized how special that gesture was, how motherly and intimate. She'd done it less for Jack than for Stone Boy, who stood to the side looking desperately at Jack. *Don't leave me*, his eyes seemed to say.

Jack turned to him. "You don't need me here. You're going to be fine. You don't understand—I have kin too. Somewhere out there." He swept his arm across the forest.

He tried to walk off, but again Stone Boy blocked his path. Jack looked into his pleading eyes, and a flood of memories overwhelmed him. His friend, his hunting companion, the boy who had saved his life. In his mind's eye he saw that mystic moonlight under which he and Stone Boy had sat leaning against each other, watching shooting stars.

Stay here, Stone Boy seemed to urge.

Jack shook his head. His gaze downcast, Stone Boy pointed between two trees to a downward slope Jack hadn't even noticed. There the forest mist seemed to brighten from a thinning in the trees.

"Thank you, Stone Boy. You know I'd take you

with me if I could, if I thought there was any chance you'd enjoy the outside world. But believe me, it's not the place for you and your kind. You might not believe this, but you're much safer here than out there." Jack stepped toward Stone Boy to embrace his friend, to wish him good-bye one last time. But just then Stone Boy dashed behind a bush and retrieved the lion paws from where he'd hidden them. He quickly made a trail of lion prints in a circle surrounding him and Jack.

Jack hesitated. "Okay," he said. "A little longer. But when I gather enough food, I'm leaving."

=‖=

ALL DAY THE TRIBE FORAGED for food, emptying one clearing and then moving to another. Alpha tore leaves off trees and clustered grubs in little mounds for the youngest members of the tribe. One of the girls foraged ahead of Jack. She chewed on some seeds and rubbed the paste onto a branch, as Alpha had done. Then she bent the branch back, loosing it smack in Jack's face. Once he recovered from the initial shock, Jack realized the girl was smiling. For some reason he smiled too, and then the smile turned to laughter, and the

207

whole tribe followed suit, laughing heartily with gentle eyes.

At dusk, Stone Boy showed Jack how to stick leafy branches in the ground and then bend them toward the center, tying up their tips, making the foliage overlap, to form a tent.

I can do this, Jack thought. *When I'm on my own, this will help.* The thought of being alone in the wild didn't scare him.

As Stone Boy's kin was about to settle in for the night, Stone Boy made a large trail of lion prints around their campsite. When he was through, he did it again, in a wider circle. By this time everyone had come out of their tents. The tribe watched Stone Boy silently, seeming to understand the safety he was offering them with this innovation. They breathed quietly and gazed at him with respect.

Jack glanced up at the canopy, scanning the branches for Mohawk, but there was no sign of him. Jack watched Stone Boy complete the circle and sidle back to the tent he'd made with Jack. Stone Boy stood taller now, holding his shoulders up, proud of his role as the tribe's protector.

When I am gone, Jack suddenly realized, *Stone Boy will lead his tribe.*

=╬=

LATER, STONE BOY LAY sound asleep. Jack wondered why sleep was nature's way of replenishing energy, since in sleep most mammals are entirely un-protected. Most animals sleep, he reflected—even ants. What makes human sleep so special? Perhaps, he thought, humans had found in sleep the unique adventure of dreams. If dreams were the soul of creativity, and creativity led to technology, inno-vation, invention, then maybe sleep was worth the risk.

Jack's mind returned to those bones in the clearing. Where was the clan headed? he won-dered. Could they survive another civil war? And how could he, the intruder, help prevent one?

His mind wandering, Jack dozed off for a few minutes but woke with a start, his heart racing. Stone Boy's warm shoulder was not leaning against his. Stone Boy, eyes glittering in the moonlight fil-tering through the canopy, sat awake, looking up, analyzing the darkness. Then, quickly, he sealed a finger over Jack's lips—hush! He shoved Jack out of the tent just as Mohawk and his gang dropped from the branches above and crushed it.

Seeing that they had missed their marks, Mohawk and his cohorts grunted angrily and gave chase. Stone Boy zigzagged through the tents, screaming, waking everyone. Then he cried out plaintively, summoning his mother. In the moonlight Jack saw Alpha rushing toward them, trying to find her son in the dark. Mohawk stopped in his tracks and gave a growl as bloodcurdling as Stone Boy's warning. All the mothers, with infants gripped to their chests, bolted from their tents, tearing them apart. In the midst of the clearing, a body writhed on the ground. "Stone Boy!" Jack yelled, but his voice was drowned by wild screeches. It wasn't Stone Boy who had fallen. On the ground, savagely kicked and bitten, one of Mohawk's followers lay still. Jack clenched his teeth so hard, his head pounded. He reached for the hunting stone, but just as he took aim at the hulks, Mohawk's horde retreated, rushing back to the trees.

Jack leaned down and gasped in relief.

The young male was whining in pain, his arms and torso bleeding all over. He must have revolted against Mohawk, or maybe even tried to hold back the raid. Now, from the trees, Mohawk screamed, shaking the forest. He threw down broken branches and spat, while the injured ape staggered to his feet, shaking his arms at his unseen leader. *I'm done with you,* he seemed to say. Stone Boy rushed to his side, as if to welcome his brother back to the fold, and patted his big arms and chest. The mothers drew back into the clearing, while Alpha shrilly barked orders. Stone Boy chattered excitedly, and Jack tried to make sense of the scene. Stone Boy pleaded to the mothers to escape, motioning to the edge of the clearing.

Noise again erupted in the branches above them. Mohawk was berating his gang, who snarled in angry response. In an instant the whole rebellious group sounded ready to shred one another. The group exploded into battle, disappearing into the forest as they gave chase to their overthrown leader.

The forest quieted. The females around Stone Boy and Jack relaxed, gradually slipping into sleep. Nestled among them, Jack didn't dare move. He felt as though he'd become one of them and, like the tribe, would do anything to survive.

AT DAWN ALPHA ROUSED her companions and barked orders. The whole tribe moved on. Alpha led the way uphill, and Stone Boy and Jack fell in line, following closely. The trail became steep, and they came to a heavily forested overlook. They had reached the highest crest in this region of the forest. Jack saw the open sky before him.

Alpha called out. The old, injured male whom Jack had spotted spying on the tribe several days earlier loped into view. He fell into step, and the whole group lumbered forward.

Just then, twigs snapped in the branches above. Jack looked up. The gang was moving with them, nearly invisible in the trees. He wondered whether Mohawk was with them. The injured old male knuckle-walked nervously with the tribe, the adult females helping him along, urging him to move faster. Alpha looked over her shoulder and saw him struggling. She slowed to give him a chance to catch up.

The tribe came upon big clusters of yellow fruit, and they stopped to eat. The fruit was sweet and pulpy and sent a rush of sugar to Jack's head. Jack tried to gauge how many fruits would fit into his Bergen. Perhaps he could slip away while the tribe was busy eating.

But something held him back. The sight of the tribe feasting happily, finally content, made him laugh. The tribe stared at him and burst into chuckles and giggles of their own. Alpha crouched down to sniff the ground, seeming to smell change in the air. Jack hoped grassland was near, where they would encounter herds of grazing herbivores. He and Stone Boy would teach them how to make spears and hunt.

When they had finished their feast, the tribe pushed forward, walking for what seemed like hours. Growing weary and weak, Jack imagined his father marching alongside him. Alan Conran was dressed in his bush outfit. His face was sweaty but determined, just the way Jack remembered him.

"How will this end, Dad?" Jack asked his father.

"You're going to make it, son," Dad replied.

Jack breathed deeply. "I want to go home."

"And you will," Dad said. Then he disappeared into the bush.

They started down another incline, headed for the grassland. Jack realized he was witnessing a turning point in the tribe's development. With Stone Boy at the forefront, they were moving from the habitat where they had thrived for years to the savanna, a place that would present them with new challenges and infinite opportunities.

Jack felt like laughing to himself, dizzy with exhaustion and hope. He remembered what Dad had told him when he had found the footprints: *Maybe you have the gift, Jack, the gift of discovery.*

Jack tripped. When he recovered from stumbling, he heard screeching from above. Mohawk dropped from the branches and stood before Alpha and Stone Boy. The whole tribe froze. Slobbering, Mohawk tried to push the tribe back, but they were already fixated by the daylight growing brighter beyond the trees. The tribe pushed past him. Approaching the border where the trees ended and the savanna began, Stone Boy shot forward, urging the tribe to cross over.

Then he looked back at Jack. *Come on*, he seemed to say.

He wants me to lead the way with him, ahead of

the others, so they'll be less frightened, Jack thought. *I'm proof that the unknown isn't always dangerous.* He turned to look at the tribe. Even Mohawk's gang was among their ranks now, while the petulant rebel was nowhere to be seen.

Jack nodded to Stone Boy, and they led the tribe into the savanna.

CHAPTER ELEVEN

The glow of the late-afternoon sun illuminated the landscape, while across the grassland, dead east, storm clouds moved across the rim. The descending sun sent long shadows over distant herds of kudus. Hippos surfaced in a nearby pond. The young females squealed in surprise. The hippos floated placidly as the girls started toward the pond, noticing the long shadows stretching from their feet. The shadows were clear and dark. The girls were incredulous, making tentative motions and watching how their shadows mimicked them.

This is it, Jack thought. *They're here now*. The tribe's steps stirred birds out of nests on the ground. In seconds, the girls were on their knees gathering fresh eggs. *They will catch up in no time*, Jack thought. The tribe didn't really need him. He wondered about teaching them to make fire, but he had lost the glass some days before. Besides, what they needed to do first was to learn to hunt and replenish their strength with hearty protein diets. Fortunately for the tribe, potential prey abounded. Antelopes were everywhere, moving into the bushes now, to be less visible to nocturnal predators.

In that first stir of night, Jack remembered all the evenings he'd spent with Stone Boy, preparing for nightfall and its dangers. Jack caught Stone Boy's eyes. He smiled, as if affirming that Jack belonged in the tribe. Only now that he was no longer an intruder did Jack feel as if he could leave. There was nothing to hold him back now—all the fears that had held him captive in this place were gone. He could finally do it alone.

"No," Jack said, shaking his head. "I have to go in the morning." He looked at his friend, self-assured and strong, leading his tribe into the future. "I belong with *my* family. But maybe I'll come back," he whispered.

The oldest male strode past, looking more confident, not fearful of the larger hominids. Glancing around, Jack counted the tribe. He reached thirty and stopped. With the plentiful food and water on the savanna, Stone Boy's tribe would grow quickly. Most of them were very young, and from the looks of it, their odds of surviving were good. Stone Boy's eyes lit up and he gestured excitedly, play-acting the motion of spearing the lion.

"Jeez, slow down." Jack laughed. "We just got here and already you want to get to work." He paused. "Okay, okay. Spears it is. Go grab a branch. I'll need a good one when I leave here anyway."

Stone Boy grinned and ran off toward a tree, where he gripped a long straight branch and snapped it from the trunk.

From out of nowhere, Mohawk appeared and yanked the branch from Stone Boy's hands. He shoved it into the smaller hominid's rib cage, making the little hunter double over in pain. Jack saw a tear in Stone Boy's flesh that looked pink for a fraction of a second, then darkened quickly with blood.

Jack dashed to Stone Boy's side and wrested the branch from Mohawk's hands. He jabbed it into Mohawk's chest, and the hulk screamed, leaping back. The tribe yowled, stunned to see blood gushing from Stone Boy's wound. They scattered, and Mohawk fell on all fours. Jack swung the branch at him but missed. Mohawk scurried back into the forest, disappearing silently. Jack put his hands under Stone Boy and tried to lift him, but Alpha pushed him aside, and in an instant the whole tribe had crowded around their fallen leader.

Alpha laid her face on Stone Boy's gashed chest, as if trying to stop the blood. He gasped and his eyelids fluttered. Alpha wailed. Other adult females dug their hands into the grass, pulled up clumps of dirt, and patted them on Stone Boy's open wound, staunching the blood.

As frightened as he was hurt, Stone Boy's head whipped around anxiously until he spotted Jack. Panicking, Jack tried to think of something helpful he could do. He remembered the fire ants. There had to be ants around here, or healing herbs. Jack remembered all the times Stone Boy had helped him, healing his arm, showing Jack how to prepare a tree for the night, building an island of grass and stone to divert the charging herd of buffaloes. Jack wiped his eyes hard and forced himself to look at the gash. The females had covered it with saliva and dirt, and now Alpha laid her cheek again on Stone Boy's heaving chest.

Stone Boy reached up to Jack and touched a tear rolling down his cheek. He looked at his friend's eyes, not understanding what he was seeing. Then Stone Boy licked his wet fingertip, still curious through all his pain.

Jack smiled through his tears. "You're going to be just fine, Stone Boy."

CHAPTER TWELVE

That night, while Stone Boy and the tribe slept beneath a full savanna moon, Jack got to work. He broke off a long, straight branch of a tree, dug a rock out of the ground, and slowly whittled the branch into a spear. Though it was difficult to see in the darkness, Jack was determined to finish his weapon before dawn.

He saw a hyena approaching and stood up, clutching the spear. The hyena backed off, either not hungry or maybe wiser than Jack gave it credit for. Jack returned to working on the spear, enjoying how the wood glinted in the moonlight.

At dawn, the sun exploded light onto the grassland. The earth warmed, and birds darted through the air. Some of the tribe snored, stirring now and then, strewn in a circle around Stone Boy. Alpha's arms were draped around her son, and her lips breathed onto his. Jack leaned in to see Stone Boy's face. He was sound asleep.

Jack moved closer. Though he was silent, Alpha sensed his presence immediately. She woke and put her lips next to Stone Boy's to see if he was breathing. She examined the wound and blew gently on his rib cage. The wound had sealed and Stone Boy seemed to be out of grave danger. The little hunter stirred.

Jack squatted beside him and eased the spear into his friend's fingers, while Alpha stared at the strange object. Stone Boy closed his fingers on it, and she looked startled.

"I want you to have it," Jack whispered. "Because I want you to live."

But Stone Boy pushed it back into Jack's hand: You *have it, I want* you *to live.*

Jack shook his head. He wanted Stone Boy

to stand up, to argue, to show Jack that he was okay.

With a great deal of effort, Stone Boy staggered up and pushed his friend away, his open palm on Jack's chest. *Go on now. I'll be fine.* Then he made a strange sound. "Ua-ta," he uttered slowly and carefully, and made a slurping sound. Stone Boy had imitated him. And the word had to be the first that Jack had uttered, thirsting in the underground lair: "Water . . . "

"Stone Boy," he whispered, amazed.

And Stone Boy pronounced it again. "Ua-ta." Sounding almost like *water*, but using the word with a new meaning: *Go away—this isn't your place.*

Jack finally took the spear and stepped backward, past the dozing tribe. He noticed a trail of decoy prints on the ground. He looked back. Alpha cradled her son, stroking his face gently. Leaning on his mother for support, Stone Boy laid himself down again. Jack took a few more steps and looked back. The tribe was stirring from sleep, yawning, blinking in the light.

He turned and faced east. The savanna lay before him. He would march into the rising sun, over the rim, and back to civilization.

He forged ahead.

Hours later, as night fell once more, the rim seemed that much closer—but ominously. Jack had a sudden sense of dread that getting out of the Witch's Pot might mean he could never return.

AFTER GATHERING MUNGONGO NUTS and camping alone, Jack woke the next day and arrived at the inner rim before the sun had reached its apex. Before starting the climb up, he paused to look for gourds or big leaves he could use to hold water. Although sizable streams flowed through cracks in the rock face, Jack knew the top of the rim would be arid and dry. He found a kind of calabash on a little tree, opened it with his spear, and poured out a greenish liquid. He cleaned out the inside with his fingers. He tasted the juice—bland. Poisonous juice was often bitter. He held the gourd in a stream and filled it to the top. He climbed up the rock face, amazed at how well he gripped the craggy surface with his feet. Halfway, he stopped, drank, and refilled his gourd from another stream.

I'll drink every time I find water, he thought, *and*

keep this gourd full. Tomorrow, if I hit a dry area, I'll have to ration it.

He went on, trying to race the sunset to the top. When the sun went down, he decided to keep climbing in the moonlight. Dust began to blow into his face, obscuring his vision.

When he pulled himself up on a ridge several hours later, sand whipped around him. He choked and tried to walk with one hand over his mouth. He looked up and saw a dust storm raging on the peaks above him. Jack tried to summon his courage and thought of Stone Boy. *I've made it this far, friend. You're going to make it too.*

Struggling with all his might against the churning, choking dust, Jack finally climbed over the inner rim. He found a crack filled with mud and scooped some onto his lips, then smeared some on his chest, arms, and thighs. This would help when the sun came up.

Delirious but determined, Jack still walked on as the morning sun blazed. He wondered how many hours had passed since he had left Stone Boy's tribe. He was off the incline now, walking across a stretch of dry, empty land. Some distance ahead lay bushes. He tried to concentrate on his feet. He could barely feel them, yet his steps pounded out a rhythm in his mind that kept him moving. Jack listened to the rhythm of his heartbeat too, adjusting his steps to match. The rhythm made the trek seem shorter, less infinite. Jack thought of time, of clocks, of how little sense he had of how many days had passed since the plane crashed.

Jack came to a lone mungongo tree. He shook the tree and gathered nuts, which he opened with his teeth. He found a puddle and drank it almost dry, and then walked on.

THAT NIGHT HE CAMPED AGAIN, and in the morning found another mungongo tree. He ate, came to another brook, drank, and walked on.

How are you, brother hunter? Jack thought. *I know you're better. Every day, you're better. I can feel it.*

Jack came to a trail of ancient footprints. He reached down to trace their outlines with his fingertips. He stood up, gazing at the petrified ash. A faint red outline circled the site—spray paint.

These were the same prints he'd discovered with Dad!

But what he saw next stopped him in his tracks. A patch of yellow paint on the ground, about six feet to one side of the trail. The paint was dry, but it was recent enough to show very clearly; it could be easily spotted, from the ground or from the sky. After Jack and Dad had found the footprints, someone else had spotted them too.

He ran around the footprints, looking for the tire tracks of a plane. But the bed of ash was hardened, and the grass around it was ravaged by hooves.

He sat down to catch his breath. Resting felt good. Jack stretched out on the ground. *Only for a few minutes*, he told himself, but when he awoke several hours later, the sun had changed position in the sky. He killed a lizard with a stone and ate it whole. Then he turned and followed the footprint trail. He began to pick up the pace, faster and faster, even after the sun had set. Pressing on, Jack was amazed—even under the stars, he could still see the outline of footprints beside him, guiding the way.

CHAPTER THIRTEEN

Jack walked on into the next day, his skin burnished from the unforgiving sun, his throat dry, his stomach empty. As he descended the face of the outer rim, Jack saw a mirage. A small airplane appeared above the horizon. *This feels very real,* Jack thought.

Then the mirage dropped altitude, its solo engine becoming so noisy that Jack felt the air shake above him. It *was* real. He started jogging toward the plane.

He saw the pilot's head emerge from the cockpit,

now only several yards above the ground. The pilot squinted his eyes and screamed something, but the engine drowned out the sound of his voice. The pilot waved his hand toward the ground. The terrain, Jack saw, was too rocky for the pilot to land. The plane circled and came back. The pilot thumbed toward the tail of the plane; then he turned and flew in that direction, waving for Jack to follow. Jack could see a hut among a cluster of trees in the distance.

He ran.

The pilot circled again, making sure that Jack was still moving toward the hut. Now the hut seemed much bigger, and the plane slowly came down on a field beside it. The little hatch door popped open, and the pilot jumped out and sprinted toward Jack. It was Frank Aoyama. Jack's legs buckled under him.

Maybe I'm dreaming, Jack told himself. But he wasn't dreaming. Frank slowed when he reached the boy. An expression of both relief and terror crossed his face.

Frank uncapped a bottle of water with his teeth and held it out. Jack sat up and took the water.

Frank asked, "You all right?"

Jack nodded and raised the bottle to his mouth. It knocked against his teeth; he made an effort to hold it firmly. He drank, lowered the bottle, and even through his fatigue almost laughed at Frank's stunned face.

"Your father? Bruce?" Frank asked, not wanting to finish the sentence. Jack shook his head.

Frank reached for Jack's wrist and took his pulse as the boy drank, water dribbling down his chin and chest. Jack realized, feeling the water on his skin, that only one piece of clothing had survived his expedition, a rag around his hips that had once been his cargo pants. The rest of his body was caked with mud and dust.

Frank gently let go of his wrist. "I just radioed the park. They're sending a helicopter. Can you talk?"

Jack nodded, and asked hoarsely, "How long was I gone?"

Something broke in Frank's expression. "Five weeks . . . I looked for you every day for two weeks before the government called off the search. They thought all of you were—" Frank bit his lower lip.

"But I kept looking, every few days. I knew something would show up. Yesterday I found a trail of fossilized footprints." Jack nodded. "There was paint on the ground. Alan had found it already?"

Jack shook his head, then pointed his thumb to his chest.

"I found it on our first day out."

Frank didn't speak for a moment. Then he cleared his voice and pointed toward the hut. It looked like a regular African house, clay adobe with a flat roof. "That's an army post," Frank explained. "I radioed them when I spotted you from the plane." As he spoke, two men appeared from the house, carrying a stretcher.

Frank took off his jacket and laid it over Jack.

"When the paramedics get here, they'll have oxygen, a glucose drip. Good news is you have a normal pulse. Jack . . . " he started. "What were you guys looking for inside the second rim?"

Jack turned and looked back: The Witch's Pot seemed to have pulled way back to the horizon, obscured in the midmorning haze.

He thought about what to say, and finally asked: "How far is that? The second rim?"

"Twenty, maybe thirty miles in. I tried to fly over it about three weeks ago—almost wrecked my plane." Jack remembered jumping up and down and yelling after he had made the fire, while that little plane struggled in the sky. So that *had* been Frank.

"Jack, that's where you were all that time?" Then Frank asked softly, "The bodies are back there?"

Jack glanced up at him.

Frank seemed to understand. He brusquely sat on the ground, realizing that it was really true: Alan was gone.

The two young men with the stretcher arrived, wearing camouflage pants and jackets without T-shirts. One of them motioned to Jack. "*Machela, machela.*"

"He says to lie on the stretcher." But Jack was too weak. Frank and the soldiers lifted him up and Jack closed his eyes. It was finally time to rest.

LATER, IN THE HUT, Jack learned the two soldiers were brothers. They had maintained this outpost for nearly two years, but Jack didn't recall flying over it. One of the men asked Frank if he could give Jack something to eat. Frank nodded. The man prepared a pot of goat's milk and cereal. Jack began to eat, while the three men hovered around him anxiously. He finished the meager meal and kept it down.

There was an old copper bathtub in the yard of the army post, which the soldiers filled with water. Frank objected to a bath before Jack was examined by a doctor, fearing that Jack's skin was too damaged. But Jack, ignoring him, stepped over the side of the tub and lowered himself into the water. The sensation of floating and the peace of mind, knowing he was finally safe, were so soothing, he soon dozed off again.

He woke when a needle pricked his arm. The paramedics' helicopter had arrived.

They checked him, rubbed disinfectant lotion on his skin, then dressed him in cutoff pants and a clean T-shirt. A smiling paramedic woman carried the IV drip as they loaded his stretcher into the helicopter. She spoke English with an American accent. "Jack, we phoned your mom in California," she said softly. "She's going to fly over on the next available plane. She'll be here as fast as she can."

Seeing Jack's relief at her words, the paramedic's eyes filled with tears. "I'm sorry," she said. "My name is Nancy Gwara. I went to one of your dad's lectures—he was so brilliant. . . . "

Jack nodded.

The helicopter's rotor blades started turning. He closed his eyes.

He lay back, and the grass swayed behind his closed eyes. For a moment he was back with the tribe. One of the youngsters loped over to Jack. Then Stone Boy ran up and pushed her aside, taking a seat beside his friend. He had the lion paws around his waist for protection. . . .

He hoped Stone Boy was all right by now.

=‖=

BACK IN THE RESEARCH center's infirmary, a doctor from the Tanzanian army took samples of Jack's blood and saliva. The nurses weighed him, cleaned him with soapy sponges, and rubbed antibacterial lotion on every little cut on his body. Nancy told him he'd have the IV drip for several days, to bring his blood sugar back to normal. The doctor checked his heart, x-rayed his chest, and took his pulse and temperature again.

"You're lucky we have pretty basic facilities here," Nancy joked. "Back in the States, we would've put you in isolation for weeks."

Frank paced, waiting for the doctor and Nancy to finish up. When they finally left, Frank came in and sat by Jack's bed, staring at the boy's bandaged feet.

"Jack, I hope you don't mind, but I mentioned the footprints to two researchers here." Jack winced. "They're men I trust with my life, and your father did too. If you feel comfortable, I'd like you to tell them your story. What you went through, how your body survived, is something of a mystery to them. To me too. Five weeks is a long time to spend alone on the savanna."

Jack looked away.

"What do you think, Jack? All right?" Jack turned back and shrugged. Frank hesitated, then walked to the door and opened it. Two young researchers stepped inside. Jack recognized them from the cantina.

"I'm André Proust," said a bearded man with a French accent. He wore the thickest glasses Jack had ever seen. "I'm the director of survival studies here."

"Jim Delmore," said the other one, holding out his hand to shake Jack's. "Geologist."

They were trying to conceal their curiosity, but Jack could sense it. Proust removed his glasses and wiped them clean on his lab coat. "The footprints you found are quite extraordinary, Jack," Proust began. "I hope you realize that. We'd like to ask your permission to lift some samples from the site. We can run a few tests at the lab and determine how old they are." He paused. "But this is your discovery. We will, of course, respect your wishes. So the sixty-four-thousand-dollar question is: What would you like us to do?"

"Do we have to report them right away?" Jack asked.

Proust shook his head.

"Jack," Delmore added, "when we do decide to go public with this, this site is going to be big news. Huge. From what Frank tells me, the prints look like the real deal—among the best preserved he's seen."

"I want to look through Dad's papers first," Jack said firmly. "I want to find out what he was working on besides the lion project."

236

"That's understandable," said Delmore. "But think about it: how you managed to survive on the savanna for so long is a story on its own. People are going to ask questions. They're going to want answers. Something to keep in mind."

Jack cleared his throat. "I need some time."

"Whenever you're ready." Proust smiled. "*Bonne chance*, eh?"

The men turned and left, closing the door behind them.

Jack glanced at Frank. "What was that about?"

"You heard them." Frank gave Jack a very straight look. "For now, it's up to you." Then he took a clear plastic bag out of his pocket. Something dark hung inside it. "Can you tell me what this is?" Frank asked, pulling a little object out of the plastic bag. He held it in his fingers. Jack looked at it.

"It's a hunting stone," he said. "Where did you find it?"

"Tucked in what's left of your Bergen. It's flaked just like the ones at Olduvai, but it's not nearly as old."

They sat for a while, neither of them speaking.

"What do you want me to do with this?" Frank finally asked, holding up the stone. Jack took it from Frank's hand and closed his fist over it.

"When you want to talk, I'm ready to listen, Jack."

"I know." Jack nodded. He turned the stone in his hand, flaked and sharp, so alive.

CHAPTER FOURTEEN

When Jack's mom stepped through the center's main door, Nancy Gwara's arm was wrapped around her, ready to catch her in case she fainted. After sleeping for three nights in the infirmary, Jack had asked to be moved into his father's study, and despite opposition from the doctor, Frank had approved. The nurses set up a cot beside Dad's desk, and more cots in the hallway for the paramedics who slept in shifts to check on Jack throughout the night.

Hearing voices outside the study, Jack sprang

out of bed and into the hallway. His mom ran toward him, looking somehow smaller than he remembered her.

"You're so skinny." Her voice broke. "Did you grow taller?" Sobbing, smiling, and hugging Jack all at once, she dropped to her knees, pulling her son down with her.

Jack kissed the top of her head reassuringly. She touched his face, his arms, his shoulders, to make sure he was all okay. "Mom, I'm fine . . . " he whispered, overcome that in this moment, she was more fragile than he was. "Why don't you come in and sit down?" he said, motioning through the door of the study.

Mom glanced past him into the room, but almost immediately she closed her eyes and turned away. "I can't go in there yet, Jack. It's just too much. Your father . . . "

Jack hugged his mom and held her tight. "I'm so sorry," he whispered. "Dad . . . he really didn't want anything bad to happen."

Mom's body shook, wracked with sobs. Jack thought maybe she understood Dad at last. She was so overwhelmed with emotion, she could barely breathe. Nancy Gwara brought her a glass of water. She drank, fanning her face and slowly catching her breath.

"Jack, if you're up to it," Nancy said softly, "we have a high school class visiting the lab here. They heard about you. Maybe I can bring them by in a few minutes?" She turned to his mom. "Of course it's up to Jack, and to you, Judy."

Mom, surprisingly, looked at Jack, nodded, and said, "Honey, it's up to you. If those kids don't tire you out . . . "

Jack looked at Nancy and nodded—she could bring in the students. Nancy stepped outside, and the kids filed into the center. They'd brought him presents—CDs, and their class book for him to sign. The kids wore white shirts and navy-blue skirts and pants. They spoke Swahili to each other, and to Jack they spoke rapid English. "What was the crash like?" was the first question, from a tall girl with a quiet face and eyes full of curiosity.

Then a skinny kid asked, "Is there going to be a movie about you?" Jack laughed.

"How did you do it?" another girl asked.

Jack had an idea. He pulled the hunting stone out of his pocket.

"I made a spear with this," he said. "I'll show you, if I can get a branch."

Frank entered, looked at Nancy, and tapped his finger on his wristwatch. Nancy nodded toward Jack's mom. But Judy didn't seem to mind; listening to Jack talk to the kids appeared to raise her spirits. Frank shrugged, and Jack led the fifth graders outside. In no time they found a tree by the cantina that had the right type of branches, low and straight. Jack pulled a branch off and set it on a nearby table. The kids held the branch down, and Jack showed them how that stone would peel the bark off and shape the spear's tip. He let them try their hands, and they took turns with the stone, giggling.

"Even if you make a really good spear, though," Jack started, "it takes a while to get the hang of aiming it. The wind can throw a spear totally off target. And sometimes when we—" Jack stopped himself. He suddenly realized how hard it was to talk about hunting, to talk about anything he had done in the past few weeks, without mentioning Stone Boy. He carefully began again. "Sometimes

242

when I sharpened my spear by holding the tip over a fire, it would get so hot, I could barely hold it."

The spear on the table had warmed up too, from all the little hands turning it, gripping it. The kids took out lunches wrapped in tin foil. *Karibu chakula!* "Come eat with us, Jack!" Jack shared a sandwich with one of the boys. Then he signed his name in their class book and wrote *Hatawa!* underneath.

After the kids had gone and Jack and his mother were walking back toward the center, the doctor intercepted them. He had run some tests on Jack's blood to determine if the boy had been exposed to any viruses or parasites in the bush. Dengue, sleeping sickness, and tick-bite fever were serious problems on the savanna.

"The results just came in, Jack," the doctor said, waving a piece of paper. Jack held his breath. "I don't know how this is possible, but they're all negative. You're completely healthy."

Mom took a deep breath. Jack smiled at her. "See? I'm fine."

With a wink, Mom ruffled his hair. "You're one tough kid." She turned back toward the center. "All right," she said. "Let's do this."

Jack took her by the hand and led her into the research building, down the long tiled hallway, and into Alan Conran's study. Overcrowded bookshelves lined one wall, stocked with anatomical texts, academic journals, and an enormous leather-bound atlas. Tucked on the shelves around the books were artifacts from Dad's adventures: a seedpod, a lion's tooth, an empty ostrich egg. Boxes full of his father's papers lay in the middle of the room beside the desk. Another wall was hung with pictures of Jack at various ages and one framed photo of his family together. In it, Jack stood between his parents in front of their old house in Pasadena.

Mom put her hand on the image. "I miss that house. We had good times there."

"I want to stay here, Mom," Jack said suddenly. Mom turned pale. "I want to know everything about Dad's research. He was looking for something out there, something besides lions. I can't explain why yet, but I need to find out what that was. Everything that happened to me started right here, in this room. Mom, I can't go back to California."

"Jack," Mom replied, taking Jack's face in her hands. "I can't imagine what you went through out there. You have no idea how close I came to losing hope that I would ever see you again. But here you are." She paused. "The doctor says you're well enough to travel. Rest up for a few more days. Then we'll go home; things will be normal again. Your friends will be so glad to see you."

"Mom," Jack said softly, "you don't understand. Dad spent his whole life trying to understand one thing: how humans developed and why. When he died, he was this close to the answer. I think I might be even closer. If we go home now, I'll never know for sure."

A look of confusion came over Mom's face. "There's so much I want to tell you, Mom." Jack clutched the stone in his pocket. "But I need time. Please?"

Mom was very still for a moment, staring at the photographs in silence. "Will you give me a minute, Jack?"

Jack nodded and slowly stepped outside, closing the door behind him. He stood in the hallway and gazed out a window, surveying the terrain that had almost killed him yet made him feel more alive than he'd ever thought possible. Sunlight shone through clouds in the distance, making them appear to glow from within. Jack couldn't imagine returning to his life in California, to pancakes on Saturdays and soccer practice after school, as long as he knew that Stone Boy's tribe was somewhere out there. He had to find his way back to them.

After what felt like forever, the door of Dad's study opened. Jack turned to his mother expectantly.

"I think," she said, "your father's office could use some new furniture. I bet Frank knows where to get a good deal on a desk around here. What do you think?"

Jack's heart jumped. "So we can stay?"

"You know," Mom began, "your dad and I disagreed on pretty much everything. But we always had faith in you. If this is what you really want, then yes, we can stay."

Jack whooped and threw his arms around his mom. "Thank you!"

"Come on," Mom said. "I'd better go unpack. We could be here for a while."

They started down the hallway. "You're going to love it here, Mom," Jack chattered excitedly. "This is going to be great."

"I don't know about that," Mom said, smiling. "I heard antelope was on the menu tonight."

Jack grinned. "Don't worry. It's a little tough at first, but you'll get used to it."

=⫶=

WALKING TO THE DORM, Jack's mom stopped suddenly as they were passing the main gate. "Oh, Jack. I can't believe it—I left my purse in your dad's office. Wait here—I'll be right back." She hurried off toward the center.

Jack leaned against a tree next to the gate and peered out into the scrub beyond it. A secretary bird high-stepped through the grass, shaking its feathered head. A group of giraffes was gathered near a tree a few hundred yards away, their necks craning to reach the top branches. The sun was setting in the west, the same direction he had flown with Dad just five weeks earlier. So much had changed since then. He felt like a completely different person than the boy who'd arrived at the center five weeks before. *What if I had never come to*

Africa? Jack wondered. *Would Dad still be alive if I had never found those footprints? But Dad would still have tried to fly over that second rim. He would surely have taken that chance, with or without me.*

And what about Stone Boy? Would Stone Boy still be wandering the savanna by himself?

Suddenly, a dark silhouette caught Jack's eye. About his size, perhaps a few inches shorter, it was moving toward him with an upright gait. Jack's heart beat wildly. Had Stone Boy followed him? At that moment the sun dropped behind the horizon and the dark silhouette was a man: Dad's friend Frank, out for a walk.

Jack smiled. Everything was okay. Somehow, in his heart, he knew Stone Boy was alive. Tomorrow the sun would be as bright and hot upon the savanna as it had been when Jack and Stone Boy hunted with spears. Soon Stone Boy and his tribe would be hunting together. Everything would be a challenge in their new habitat, probably for years to come. But gradually, as humans had done for ages, they would adjust, learn, evolve. They would survive.

ACKNOWLEDGMENTS

A book makes friends while it's being written—friends who read drafts and take the time to give opinions and encouragement. Their help is invaluable. I got help from Keith, Jack, Trevor, Jordy, Sammy, Matthew, and Julian, boys who meet every week to read and discuss books on my own street. They were the first with whom I shared chapters about Stone Boy's adventures, and about how Stone Boy helped Jack, my thirteen-year-old hero, to be rescued in the African savanna. What good times we had, I and my first seven readers.

To Laura Geringer, who helped me come up with the concept of this series, and Lindsey Alexander and Jill Santopolo, who edited it expertly, I owe some of my first steps in the children's book genre. Thank you so much. To my wife, Iris, my son, Adam, and daughter, Chloe, I owe, of course, my survival during the writing adventure—thank you, thank you, for saving my life! John Silbersack, my agent at Trident Media Group, helped at all turns in the adventure and taught me how to go better prepared into the wild next time. Joyce Rappaport, a good friend, reread the material when it was done. I thank you all, again.

Petru Popescu
Los Angeles, 2007